A moving sh
warning the

Bolan did a full running roll to get out of the way as a machete glinted in the moonlight.

“Got to kill you,” the heavily accented voice said. “For the Obeah Man.”

Bolan kept moving and came up with the Desert Eagle in his hand. He needed someone left alive who could talk, so he fired low, blowing out the man’s kneecap.

The posse member screamed and went down, and Bolan immediately turned back to the driveway, hoping to catch up to his target. But the car kicked up gravel as it peeled away, and he got only a glimpse inside—enough to see that the Obeah Man was getting away.

Bolan walked back to the man screaming on the ground and kicked the machete out of reach. “We need to have a talk.”

“Screw you!” the man muttered.

“It’s a start,” the Executioner said. “But I’m looking for something a little more informative.”

MACK BOLAN®
The Executioner

#320 Exit Code
#321 Suicide Highway
#322 Time Bomb
#323 Soft Target
#324 Terminal Zone
#325 Edge of Hell
#326 Blood Tide
#327 Serpent's Lair
#328 Triangle of Terror
#329 Hostile Crossing
#330 Dual Action
#331 Assault Force
#332 Slaughter House
#333 Aftershock
#334 Jungle Justice
#335 Blood Vector
#336 Homeland Terror
#337 Tropic Blast
#338 Nuclear Reaction
#339 Deadly Contact
#340 Splinter Cell
#341 Rebel Force
#342 Double Play
#343 Border War
#344 Primal Law
#345 Orange Alert
#346 Vigilante Run
#347 Dragon's Den
#348 Carnage Code
#349 Firestorm
#350 Volatile Agent
#351 Hell Night
#352 Killing Trade
#353 Black Death Reprise
#354 Ambush Force
#355 Outback Assault
#356 Defense Breach
#357 Extreme Justice
#358 Blood Toll
#359 Desperate Passage
#360 Mission to Burma
#361 Final Resort
#362 Patriot Acts
#363 Face of Terror
#364 Hostile Odds
#365 Collision Course
#366 Pele's Fire
#367 Loose Cannon
#368 Crisis Nation
#369 Dangerous Tides
#370 Dark Alliance
#371 Fire Zone
#372 Lethal Compound
#373 Code of Honor
#374 System Corruption
#375 Salvador Strike
#376 Frontier Fury
#377 Desperate Cargo
#378 Death Run
#379 Deep Recon
#380 Silent Threat
#381 Killing Ground
#382 Threat Factor
#383 Raw Fury
#384 Cartel Clash
#385 Recovery Force
#386 Crucial Intercept
#387 Powder Burn
#388 Final Coup
#389 Deadly Command
#390 Toxic Terrain
#391 Enemy Agents
#392 Shadow Hunt
#393 Stand Down
#394 Trial by Fire
#395 Hazard Zone

The Don Pendleton's

Executioner®

HAZARD ZONE

PAPL
DISCARDED

TORONTO • NEW YORK • LONDON
AMSTERDAM • PARIS • SYDNEY • HAMBURG
STOCKHOLM • ATHENS • TOKYO • MILAN
MADRID • WARSAW • BUDAPEST • AUCKLAND

If you purchased this book without a cover you should be aware that this book is stolen property. It was reported as "unsold and destroyed" to the publisher, and neither the author nor the publisher has received any payment for this "stripped book."

Recycling programs
for this product may
not exist in your area.

First edition October 2011

ISBN-13: 978-0-373-64395-0

Special thanks and acknowledgment to
Dylan Garrett for his contribution to this work.

HAZARD ZONE

Copyright © 2011 by Worldwide Library

All rights reserved. Except for use in any review, the reproduction or utilization of this work in whole or in part in any form by any electronic, mechanical or other means, now known or hereafter invented, including xerography, photocopying and recording, or in any information storage or retrieval system, is forbidden without the written permission of the publisher, Worldwide Library, 225 Duncan Mill Road, Don Mills, Ontario, Canada M3B 3K9.

This is a work of fiction. Names, characters, places and incidents are either the product of the author's imagination or are used fictitiously, and any resemblance to actual persons, living or dead, business establishments, events or locales is entirely coincidental.

® and TM are trademarks of the publisher. Trademarks indicated with ® are registered in the United States Patent and Trademark Office, the Canadian Trade Marks Office and in other countries.

Printed in U.S.A.

Everyone has his superstitions. One of mine has always been when I started to go anywhere, or to do anything, never turn back or to stop until the thing intended was accomplished.

—Ulysses S. Grant
1822–1885

Each mission has its challenges, and the path to resolution is never predictable. But regardless of the hurdles, I promise to always follow through until every last enemy is taken care of...one way or another.

—Mack Bolan

THE MACK BOLAN LEGEND

Nothing less than a war could have fashioned the destiny of the man called Mack Bolan. Bolan earned the Executioner title in the jungle hell of Vietnam.

But this soldier also wore another name—Sergeant Mercy. He was so tagged because of the compassion he showed to wounded comrades-in-arms and Vietnamese civilians.

Mack Bolan's second tour of duty ended prematurely when he was given emergency leave to return home and bury his family, victims of the Mob. Then he declared a one-man war against the Mafia.

He confronted the Families head-on from coast to coast, and soon a hope of victory began to appear. But Bolan had broken society's every rule. That same society started gunning for this elusive warrior—to no avail.

So Bolan was offered amnesty to work within the system against terrorism. This time, as an employee of Uncle Sam, Bolan became Colonel John Phoenix. With a command center at Stony Man Farm in Virginia, he and his new allies—Able Team and Phoenix Force—waged relentless war on a new adversary: the KGB.

But when his one true love, April Rose, died at the hands of the Soviet terror machine, Bolan severed all ties with Establishment authority.

Now, after a lengthy lone-wolf struggle and much soul-searching, the Executioner has agreed to enter an "arm's-length" alliance with his government once more, reserving the right to pursue personal missions in his Everlasting War.

Prologue

"Shiver shot!" everyone screamed at once, laughing and giggling.

Bastiene "Spook" Durene smiled at the group of college students seated around the table, while the young woman to his right blushed. For their evening entertainment, they'd chosen a popular drinking game called Suicide Kings, and with some subtle manipulation of the cards, he'd drawn the King of Spades.

They were far too drunk to realize he'd been stacking the deck all night, moving the game to the outcome he desired, while ensuring his own sobriety. There was too much to accomplish this night to allow himself to become inebriated. Bastiene pointed a long finger at the woman, then picked up a thin wedge of lime from the bowl on the table. "You," he said, pitching his voice low enough so that only she could hear him.

"Me," she said, blushing again as he placed the lime between her lips. She grasped it between her teeth.

He leaned closer, then slowly ran his tongue along her neck. She shivered and he smiled once more, hiding his grin beneath a long curl of her hair. Everything was going according to plan. He reached for the saltshaker and tossed a few shakes at the damp line he'd put on her neck, then he licked it clean, drank off the shot of tequila and moved to her lips. He took the lime from her mouth into his, turning it into a deep kiss.

"Mmm," he whispered against her neck as the kiss ended. "I be bettin' you *glamity* tastes even finer." Bastiene purposely used the Jamaican accent and slang she and her friends expected, though he could, and often did, speak perfect English.

"Glamity?" she asked, giggling.

"I be showin' you soon," he said. "And you be showin' me."

The young woman laughed and leaned away. Her name was Amber Carson. Tall and seductive, she had a body that would make any frat boy her willing slave. She pushed a strand of her blond hair over her shoulder as she moved the shot glasses out of the way. So far, she'd already had six shots of from the large bottle of tequila. This night, all his work would pay off. This was Amber's fourth trip to Jamaica, and each time, he'd made a point of meeting her, getting to know her a little bit better. He tried not to laugh as she even now had to puzzle over the true meaning of his words.

He watched as she grasped what he meant—that she would taste good in her most private of places—then openly grinned as her blush deepened even more. "Maybe," she said, laughing and pushing him away. "And maybe not! First I've got to get something to eat!"

"Then let's get you something to eat," he said, gesturing at the nearby buffet table that was loaded with food.

Her chair scraped the floor as she rose unsteadily to her feet. "Deal me out," she said. "It's food or puke, and I'm voting with my feet."

Everyone laughed again and waved her off as she headed

to the buffet. Bastiene followed closely behind her. In the times she'd been here, he'd learned a great deal about her. Her father was a U.S. senator, but before that, he'd built a pretty sizable fortune in various types of mining. She was obviously spoiled—how many young women got to spend their downtime at a private resort in Jamaica—but he also knew she was just a year away from finishing her undergraduate degree in international law in the top ten of her class. He'd even overheard her talking with her friends about graduate school and someday working in a U.S. Embassy somewhere overseas.

With her connections, such a dream would be attainable. If Bastiene had any truly compassionate feelings at all, he might feel a little sad that her dream would never come true. Unfortunately for her, he didn't feel much compassion for anyone, let alone a spoiled little rich girl who was merely one cog in a much bigger plan. The world was filled with young women like her, and one more or less would make no difference.

The Goldshore Villas Resort was a custom-built haven for the rich and the privileged. The private condominium community was especially popular this time of year, when wealthy kids from the U.S. came to Montego Bay for spring break. With private hot tubs and lots of hidden paths for secret trysts, it was the perfect place to escape the notice of overprotective parents and the prying eyes of paparazzi that hounded them in the States. For this trip, Amber had brought a half-dozen friends with her, and they lived it up in a style that would make most of the other students in Jamaica for the weeklong party green with envy. There was plenty of booze, mountains of food and enough ganja to keep everyone happily stoned. When they weren't playing in the surf or lying on the beach, they were dancing and partying and having sex.

Bastiene was one of a handful of locals who knew her

well—and he'd made it a point of being one of the few who always showed up to party on his off-hours. His time working here was almost done, however, and he was grateful for that. She was the one, the Obeah man had assured him, that would allow their plans to move into the next and final phase. They would finally be ready.

Amber stopped at the buffet, picked up a plate and began to load it with fruit and cheese. She glanced over her shoulder at him as she continued along the line feigning interest that was even less subtle with her overindulgence of tequila. He knew she was checking to see if he'd followed. From what he'd overheard on her first day there, she'd just broken up with a fairly serious boyfriend, and was committed to having a commitment-free but very fun weekend. He'd turned on the charm after that, using his dark good looks and deep voice to every advantage. He had some fun in mind, too. The mission was important, but there was no reason not to indulge in the little slice of American pie, especially after all of his hard work.

Adjusting his dreadlocks, he moved behind her and put his large hands on her shoulders, rubbing gently. She leaned back into him, rubbing seductively. He kissed her neck just behind her ear.

She giggled once more, and he leaned close to whisper, "What's so funny, girl?"

"Nothing I'm willing to share yet," she said archly, turning her attention back to the buffet. She loaded up a plate with jerk chicken, seasoned rice and coco bread. "Come sit with me?" she asked.

"Of course," he said, gesturing to a small, private table beneath an umbrella, then leading the way to pull out her chair. "Something to drink?" he asked as she sat down.

"Just a cola," she said. "If I'm going to last the night, I need to slow down a little."

He nodded and crossed the patio to the wet bar, slipping

behind it to get her cola. With his hands hidden by the front of the bar, he slipped the small vial of white powder from his pocket. He tapped the vial with the roofie to keep it from sticking in the humid Jamaican climate and poured it into the glass. After adding a few cubes of ice and filling it with cola, he used a swizzle stick from the bar to mix it carefully, ensuring that the powder had dissolved completely. Then he returned to the table where she had made a sandwich from the jerk chicken on the coco bread.

"Ask and receive," he said, offering her the glass.

She took it from his hand, then gulped down several large swallows. "Thanks," she said. "I was getting a little dehydrated."

"I understand," he said. "Eat and you'll feel better."

She resumed her meal and he watched her carefully, noting how often she drank from the glass, and seeing the drug slowly take effect. "I must have had…" she started to say, her words slurring as she verbally stumbled. She tried again, laughing. "More tequila than I thought."

"Don' you worry on it," he said. "Jus' relax and everything gonna be fine."

Amber turned and stared into his eyes. "You're…beautiful," she said. "You have a voice like…like…melted chocolate."

"Thank you," he said. "You are beautiful, too."

She finished off the cola and the food, and tried to get to her feet. It was only by moving quickly that he was able to catch her and keep her from falling flat on her rear end. "Oops!" she said.

"Perhaps you should be lying down," he suggested, holding her tightly in his arms.

"Is that an offer?" She laughed.

"It is," he said.

"Then take me to my room!" she demanded, pointing back at the resort and swaying on her feet. In another few minutes, the drug would rapidly overcome her system. He needed to move quickly.

"Ask and receive," he said again, scooping her off her feet completely.

"Whee!" she cried.

Her friends turned to see the commotion and laughed. "Hey, Amber," one of her girlfriends shouted. "Are you off to explore the dark continent?" Laughter echoed over the patio again.

"Every...single...inch!" she crowed. "Got to sample the local cuisine!"

He smiled broadly and began carrying her toward the resort building where her condo was located. In less time than it took him to get there, she was passed out completely. Before he got to the building itself, he turned and made his way around the side. No one was in sight, and he moved to the front and to the waiting Jeep.

Another man got out and opened the back. He put Amber's unconscious form inside. "Take her to the Obeah man," he said. "She is not to be harmed. I will be there as soon as I can."

"You got it," the other man said. He jumped back in, started the engine, then drove away.

Bastiene returned to the main building and made his way to Amber's room. Once there, he checked to ensure that her bed looked slept in—it did—and that nothing else was out of place. He took a glass from the bar and poured a generous serving of rum. He wandered around the room as he sipped his drink. A mirror next to the dresser showed the red lipstick smudge on his collar. He moved to the wet bar and sat quietly for several minutes finishing off the rum. When he was done, he put it back on the bar and headed out of the room.

He took his time, walking calmly, and arrived back at the patio. Amber's girlfriend—a redhead whose name he didn't know—laughed uproariously when he explained sheepishly that she'd passed out before the explorations could begin. "Perhaps I'll do better tomorrow," he said.

"Not if she's sober!" the young woman replied.

Everyone laughed, including Bastiene, and he made a point of staying for several more hours, then excusing himself for the night. On his way out, he stopped by the front desk and chatted with the clerk for several minutes, then he went out the front door, got into his own Jeep and left.

On his way to the hidden home of the Obeah man, he scrubbed away the makeup on his face and arms that hid the tattoos and scars marking him as a member of the Undead Posse…and an apprentice to the Obeah arts.

"THIS PART IS CRITICAL, man," Bastiene said. "The trigger must not move until the autopsy."

The little man with the wire-rimmed glasses nodded. "I know, I know," he said. "I've got my orders."

On the slab before him was the body of Amber Carson. The drug Bastiene had given her had done its work well. Half-conscious, she was almost unresisting as he'd raped her. The Obeah man had said that his seed would be the magic that ensured their success. As far as Bastiene was concerned, magic or not, taking the young woman had been a pleasure. Her body had been warm and supple, her breasts firm. The way she'd squirmed and wriggled beneath him in protest had added greatly to the experience. Even in death she was still beautiful, the perfect corpse, looking almost alive, a siren drawing in its prey.

After, it had been a matter of little work to smother her to death, then mark the body with his thin-bladed knife. This final step, however, was crucial. The little man was Dr. Steffens, and he'd been sent by the man helping them in the United States to perform a special surgery. Using a tiny camera and going in through her esophagus, Steffens was placing two items in Amber's abdominal cavity. The first was a thin metal tube filled with anthrax spores, and the second was a unique triggering mechanism.

When the doctor performing the autopsy in the United States made the initial incisions to open her up, the mechanism would be armed by the change in internal pressure. Then, when he delved farther to explore her internal organs—specifically her stomach—the trigger would be released by this second change in pressure. The resulting small explosion would tear a hole in the metal tube, spilling the anthrax spores into the room and killing everyone present.

If it worked.

The double pressure switch had to be positioned perfectly next to the tube, and also resistant to the natural gases that would build up in her body as it decomposed and the pressure changes that would occur when her body was flown back to the United States. Finding the perfect methodology had been a matter of numerous experiments, conducted in extreme secrecy. Once they'd finalized their technique, they needed to decide on a target.

It had been their friend in the United States who had suggested Amber—young, beautiful and a senator's daughter. Her body would be flown back to Washington, D.C., and treated with the utmost care. Taking the job at the private resort where she came to play had been a hassle, but the Obeah man often told Bastiene that the best magic came from association with the victim. It was unfortunate that he'd have to continue to work there for some time afterward—it was the only way to avoid being accused—and even then, suspicions would be high. There was always a price to be paid for such powerful magic, and if he needed to still play serving boy then he would do so.

Steffens mumbled something under his breath, then let out a long, slow exhale and leaned back.

"What?" Bastiene demanded. "Is there a problem?"

"No," Steffens said. "She's ready. Just be sure not to bounce her around too much when you move her."

"I'll be as soft as a lamb," he said.

"Good," the man replied. "Then I'm out of here. There's a chopper waiting to take me back to my ship."

"Go, man," Bastiene said, gesturing toward the door. "I'll be takin' care of the girl."

Other than imminent violence, few things had the power to bring Mack Bolan, aka the Executioner, fully awake like a phone call in the middle of the night. As the first tones sounded from his cell phone, he sat up in bed, aware that these calls never came with good news—usually just the opposite. Someone was either dead or someone needed to be.

"Yeah," he said, answering before the second ring had finished.

"Sorry to wake you, Striker."

He recognized the voice of Hal Brognola immediately. Brognola was the director of the Sensitive Operations Group—located at Stony Man Farm, Virginia. He used to work for the clandestine organization directly, but now had an arm's length association with the outfit. Their mission hadn't changed—they still took on terrorists and criminals that the U.S. government couldn't or wouldn't. When the situation was complicated, they called on Mack Bolan to uncomplicate it. His presence was never official.

"It's not a problem, Hal," he said. "What's going on?"

"We've got a full-scale mess," he said. "There's been an anthrax attack in Washington, D.C. It's been contained, but a senator was killed, and the whole thing is getting ready to turn into an epic disaster."

Bolan knew the security precautions that had been in place since 9/11. "That's a mess all right. How'd they get anthrax that close to a U.S. senator?"

"You won't believe me when I tell you," Brognola said. "It was stored inside the body of his dead daughter. Somehow, these terrorists rigged it to explode during the autopsy—and, of course, Senator Carson demanded to be on hand."

"What?" Bolan was rarely disturbed by the things he saw and heard, but this was going too far. "Her body exploded?"

"Apparently it was some kind of pressure trigger," Brognola explained. "When they got to her stomach…"

"Jesus," Bolan said.

"Yeah, I know. It's unheard-of, and the kind of play that only truly bad men would even consider. The entire thing is on video, and it will be in the file I'm sending. Anyway, Senator Carson was killed, along with his Secret Service agent, the doctor and his assistant, and several other people who ran into the room after the explosion. This was weaponized anthrax, Stricker. They've had to seal off an entire section of Bethesda Naval Hospital, and the other bodies in the morgue were contaminated, too. The whole place has to go through decon."

"I assume you want me to track down the source of the attack?"

"Yeah, that and…" Brognola's voice trailed off.

"And what?" Bolan asked. "Come on, Hal, you don't usually hesitate."

The big Fed sighed heavily. "Look, this wasn't just a well-executed biological attack. They used her, Striker, and I mean that in the most literal sense. The coroner had already completed the rape kit and some of the toxicology before the explosion. She'd been given Rohypnol. She was raped and killed. Symbols had been carved into her body with some kind of thin-bladed knife. And then they filled her with a deadly virus and killed her father, along with some other good people. I don't just want the source, Striker. I want to know every bastard that was behind this and..."

Bolan could hear the deep anger in Brognola's voice, and he felt some of it himself. "What exactly do you want me to do, Hal?"

"I want you to do whatever it takes," he snapped. "I want the son of a bitch responsible for this to pay. The full tab."

"All right," he said. "Where do I start?"

"Looks like you're going back to Jamaica," Brognola said. "Amber Carson was down there on vacation. I'll send you over everything we've got on her. You've been booked on a flight leaving in—" Bolan could hear the clicking of a keyboard in the background "—five-and-a-half hours."

"What's my cover?" Bolan asked.

"I know you prefer something less flashy, but I'm going to send you in as CIA, and I'll get you a meet at the American Embassy in Kingston. Amber's death has already created a shitstorm down there, and it's a guarantee that every government agency we've got is going to have people traipsing around. One more agent asking questions should go unnoticed, but still get you a little cooperation."

"I don't know that *traipsing* is the word. With a dead senator, you won't be able to move five feet without running into some government official from here or there. Our deal is usually low profile, and this has the makings of a very high-profile mess. Why is Stony Man Farm so quick to jump in when there are so many other agencies involved?" Before Brognola could respond, he added, "Look, I understand it's bad, what they did to the girl, and the anthrax, even the death of a senator, but that doesn't automatically make it one for us."

"Striker, I know," Brognola said. "It's... Yeah, this one is a little personal, I get that, but it's well within our mandate."

Bolan considered his friend's words. "And you're sure this is how you want to play it, Hal?"

"I'm sure, Striker," he said. "I *need* you on this one. I can't trust that anyone else will do it right, and I don't want there to be some kind of cover-up if this gets really big."

"All right," he said. "I'll find whoever did this, Hal."

"I know you will, Striker. Good luck." Brognola ended the connection.

Bolan put his phone back on the nightstand and headed for the shower. It was going to be a long day, and he wanted to review the file Brognola was sending to him before he got on the plane, as well as review anything the news might have on the situation.

As he stepped under the hot spray of the shower and leaned into the pressure of the water, Bolan couldn't keep the disturbing thought of how brutal it was to kill a man's daughter and then use the grief to kill the parent, as well. There was a lot of evil in the world, but this was a level of brutality that didn't come around too often.

He decided it wouldn't hurt to do some research online. He'd run across some Jamaican gangbangers in the past, and they played hardball. He also had a recent run-in with chemical zombies in Jamaica. But biological weapons didn't seem to fit with anything the gangs had done before. Any intel he could come up with before he went in might be a weapon he could use later.

And Bolan had the feeling that he'd need every weapon he could get.

SITTING IN FRONT of his laptop, Bolan reviewed the file Brognola had sent, then went online and used the instructions the big Fed had given him in order to view the video file of what happened at Amber Carson's autopsy. It had been stored behind several federal law-enforcement firewalls, but Aaron Kurtzman and the cyberteam at Stony Man Farm had no trouble finding work-arounds to get him in.

The video showed the autopsy suite at Bethesda Naval Hospital. On the stainless-steel table, a beautiful young woman was covered with a sheet. Nearby, the coffin in which she'd been transported back to the States sat on a table, the lid open. Bolan froze the image and saw that the coffin was metal and stamped with the seal of the Coast Guard. That explained why the trigger, which had to have been pressure based, didn't activate prior to the autopsy—the coffin had been pressurized and sealed to preserve evidence.

He tapped the play icon and the video resumed. Standing over the body of Amber Carson was a man who spoke into the hanging microphone, identifying himself as Dr. Harvey Palfrey. He gave the particulars of her name and date of birth, while across the room, a sad-faced man Bolan recognized as Senator William Carson stood and watched. Next to him, a Secret Service agent stared at nothing, while occasionally speaking into his wrist microphone to update the other agents that were undoubtedly outside the room. Reading from a sheet of notes, Palfrey gave the findings of the already completed toxicology report and the rape kit.

Bolan felt a thread of anger burn in his stomach. Amber Carson had been young, beautiful and well educated, with a world of opportunity in front of her. She should have lived a long, full life. Now she was dead—raped and murdered by some thug. He also felt badly for Dr. Palfrey. As one of the handful of physicians at Bethesda Naval Hospital who regularly served members of Congress, it was his unfortunate task to conduct the autopsy. Under normal circumstances, performing an autopsy on a young person was undoubtedly unpleasant; with Senator William Carson watching as he did so, would have made any doctor tense.

Bolan froze the video on Carson's face. The poor man

obviously hadn't slept in several days, and it was a little strange that he'd be present for the autopsy itself. Still, he was a grieving father, and a powerful Senator, so if he'd made an issue of being there, even Dr. Palfrey couldn't rightly gainsay him. He started the video once more and listened as Palfrey asked the senator again if he would consider waiting outside. Carson frowned and shook his head.

"Please, Senator," Dr. Palfrey said. "I understand—"

"Enough!" he snapped. "I want the answers. Nothing is going to happen unless I am around to see it. I wasn't there when she died, but I sure as hell am going to find out who did this and make them pay. You and I both know that nothing in Washington is a coincidence, and I don't believe that the daughter of a senator is killed this way by happenstance."

Senator Carson moved forward and instinctively Palfrey moved back. Bolan watched as Carson stretched out his hand and stroked his daughter's blond hair. The pain seemed to almost overwhelm him as he leaned on the table with his other hand. The room stayed silent for another minute. Palfrey finally broke the silence by clearing his throat. The senator straightened and turned on his heel to return to his place next to the Secret Service agent.

"Get on with it. The sooner you're finished, the sooner we can have the full findings. I flew to Jamaica to pick up her body, and I will stand by her until she is properly laid to rest. It is…it is the least I can offer her until the raping, murderous son of a bitch who did this to her can be brought to justice."

The doctor's shoulders slumped in defeat, but he nodded and resumed his position next to the table.

Not knowing the man, Bolan couldn't make a guess as to Carson's motivations, but he was obviously obsessed with knowing everything—and if everything was horrible and disturbing, it would likely only further fuel his rage and insistence on justice.

Palfrey turned his attention to the body on the table and lowered the boom microphone, then selected a scalpel from the tray next to him. Lifting up the vital-statistics card, he started the official recording, giving Amber's name and statistics, then turned to the body. "Beginning the initial incision, a standard Y cut to prepare the chest and abdominal cavities."

He worked quickly, speaking his findings into the microphone as he went. An assistant stood nearby, making notes and moving in clean containers for the organs when they were needed. Carson and the Secret Service agent stood silently, flinching only when they used a small saw to get past the rib cage. The doctor examined and removed Amber's lungs, kidneys, spleen and liver, noting that each appeared healthy and undamaged.

"Moving on to the intestinal tract and the stomach," Palfrey said. He made another incision, angling the cut slightly to avoid slicing open the stomach until he'd removed it from the abdominal cavity. "The appearance of the stomach organ is—" he started to say, then stopped. "Did anyone else hear that?" he asked.

Bolan could detect a barely audible high-pitched whine, and he saw the Secret Service agent begin to move.

Then the stomach exploded in Palfrey's hands, and he screamed in agony. The video captured the flash of powder-filled light and then stopped.

"Damn," Bolan muttered, knowing that the attack was not only vicious, but required genuine imagination and intelligence. He closed the file and finished packing. He had a flight to catch and some very bad men to track down and bring to justice.

The American Embassy in Jamaica was a diplomat's dream. Located in the center of Kingston in a converted hotel, it towered over the surrounding neighborhoods, with gleaming white walls and windows on every floor. Bolan was reminded of many of the older towns in Europe and the Middle East, where the community developed around a central fortress.

As Bolan stepped out of his rental car, the humid Jamaican air filled his lungs. After showing his credentials to the well-armed Marines stationed at the front gate, he'd been waved through and found a lone parking spot far enough away to guarantee he'd be covered in sweat by the time he got inside the building. He grabbed his briefcase and headed toward the front entrance.

The soldier stepped into the lobby with a sense of relief, the humid air having made quick work of soaking his clothing, evident as he tried to pull the damp material away from his skin. The air-conditioning was going full blast. He'd been here before and in enough similar environments to know how to tolerate the humidity, but that didn't keep him from appreciating cooler air. He moved to the reception desk and displayed his credentials to the blond-haired receptionist. "Matt Cooper for Conrad Anders," he said.

The young woman behind the desk visibly flinched when Bolan flashed the CIA badge. He was curious about the reaction. CIA agents tended to make people a little nervous, but the look in her eyes was more "scared rabbit" than "what's he know about me that I wish he didn't?"

"Oh…yes, sir. He's expecting you, sir."

"Good," he replied. "Where will I find him?"

"His office is on the second floor. Take the stairs, turn right and go straight down the hall. You can't miss it." She gestured with one well-manicured hand to the double-wide staircase that had once led to the mezzanine level of the hotel but now led to offices.

Deciding to test his suspicions, Bolan leaned over the desk slightly, his size and direct gaze causing her to flinch again. "Thank you," he said. "But I'm curious. Is there a problem I should be aware of? You seem…nervous."

She shook her head so rapidly that her hair came loose from its pins and formed a swirling cloud around her head. "No, sir," she said rapidly. "I'm…I'm just new here and not used to everything yet. And we've been particularly busy with the death of Senator Carson's daughter. The phone hasn't stopped ringing."

He leaned back and glanced at the nameplate on the desk. "Then you should try to relax, Anna. CIA agents are government employees, just like you."

"Yes, sir," she said. "But I don't carry a gun or have… secrets."

"Everyone has secrets, Anna," he replied, then turned away.

Still thinking that her behavior was a bit strange, Bolan headed up the stairs, checking that the Desert Eagle was secure in its holster. Something was off with this place, he could feel it, and he wasn't about to get taken by surprise.

The stairs and hallway were carpeted in a deep red shag that went halfway up the walls, and the effect was somewhat disconcerting. It looked as if he was walking on a river of blood. He reached the end of the hallway and saw that Anders warranted a receptionist of his own, though unlike the blonde downstairs, this lady was in her late twenties or early thirties, with skin as dark as coffee, and thick, heavy braids in her hair.

"Agent Cooper?" she asked as he approached. "Mr. Anders is expecting you. I'll take you right in."

When she stood up, Bolan saw that even in heels, she barely reached his chin. She wore a floral sundress that clung to her body in all the right places, and the effect was obviously intentional. She moved to the closed door, opened it and gestured for him to enter. Bolan walked in and paused as the door clicked shut behind him.

Conrad Anders stood up from his desk and crossed to the middle of the room. Bolan recognized the posture and the frown—a stance that said, "This is *my* sandbox." Standing a good six foot two and built like a brick outhouse, Anders was a formidable enough figure to give most men pause. But Bolan wasn't most men and had very little use for men who proclaimed their territory like a rooster. In his experience, most of them were as full of hot air as the Jamaican countryside.

"Agent Cooper," Anders said, offering his hand. "Welcome to Jamaica."

"Interesting," he replied, shaking hands. "I'm not sure *welcome* is the right word."

Anders sighed and nodded. "Sorry about that. The truth is that I'm hoping you can explain to me some of the cloak-and-dagger crap I've been getting fed since this mess with Amber Carson started. To tell you the truth, the bullshit is starting to pile up, taste bad and stink to high heaven."

This guy might not like him playing in his sandbox,

Bolan thought, but at least he wasn't going to play the political game. Maybe his initial pose had been one he'd adopted due to the situation, rather than his normal way of acting.

"You know the drill, then," Bolan replied, "and you won't be surprised when I tell you that explanations are not going to be forthcoming anytime soon. About all I can offer is what you already know—we're looking into Amber Carson's murder."

"You and everyone else, Agent Cooper," Anders said. "But now I've heard that there was some kind of explosive planted in her body that killed her father."

"That was supposed to be a secret," he said. "You must have good sources, because it's true."

"I'm the intelligence officer for this embassy," he said. "But my sources have less to do with it than the fact that we're in Jamaica. Keeping secrets here is like telling a four-year-old not to tell Mommy or Daddy. It's a guarantee they'll talk. This place is rife with rumor and speculation."

"It must make separating the truth from the lies more difficult."

Anders shrugged. "That's part of my job. The sad thing is that with so much trouble in the region, there's almost always some shred of truth to the rumors. Leads are difficult to track down because the culture here makes deciphering meaning almost impossible. Just when you think you've pinned something or someone down, you find out you've been on a trail that leads to nowhere. And now with a senator dead, getting anything useful will be twice as hard." He moved to look out the window.

"Sounds frustrating," Bolan said. "But what can you tell me that I need to know before I go looking for answers?"

"What you really need to know about are the posses. Everything else is just window dressing."

"Posses?" he asked, playing dumb. "Like the Old West?"

"No," Anders said, chuckling. "The posses are Jamaican

gangs, but unlike most of the inner-city thugs you see in the U.S., these guys are organized and revered. They control the neighborhoods with money, drugs, weapons, you name it. The police don't have half their power or influence, and the posses actually wield political power because they control the people here."

"How likely is it that one of these posses was involved in Amber Carson's death?"

"Very likely," Anders said. "Almost guaranteed."

He reached for a file on his desk. Flipping through the pages, he opened to a picture of a body in a morgue. Centered in the frame was a tattoo on the right arm of the deceased—a grim reaper cradling a skull. "Take a look at this," he said. "The Undead Posse."

"They sound charming," Bolan said. "Why are they called the Undead Posse?"

"If you ask the locals," Anders replied, "it's because their leader is actually one of the living dead."

"Really," Bolan said, handing the folder back to Anders. "The living dead?"

"I'm not kidding," he said. "You've heard of voodoo, yes?"

Bolan nodded. In fact he was all too familiar.

Anders tossed the folder back onto his desk. "The locals believe that this new posse, the Undead Posse, is being led by some kind of..." He shrugged. "I don't even know what the hell to call it. Someone back from the dead, but not a zombie or a vampire. Or maybe it's a zombie. Who the hell knows?"

"Tell me about the posses in general," Bolan replied.

Anders returned to his desk and sat down, gesturing for Bolan to do the same. "Like I told you, they're gangs, but better run than anything I've ever heard about in the U.S. They run drugs, mostly, here and in the U.S. Very big in Miami, New York and up into Canada. But they're willing to fight with automatic weapons over turf—drive-bys are common—and they don't fear law enforcement at all."

"Why are they tolerated?" Bolan asked, thinking of all the various forms of organized crime that he'd rooted out over the years.

"Because they're everywhere," Anders replied simply. "They outnumber law enforcement, have more money and better guns. When arrests are attempted, the people riot in the streets because the posses supply them with drugs, food, money and protection."

"So why do you think this Undead Posse was involved in Amber Carson's murder?" Bolan said.

"The dead man in the picture," he said. "That tattoo is their symbol. He was found near the resort where she was staying. His throat had been cut."

"Professional or personal?" Bolan asked.

"Probably both," Anders replied. "The posses hand out their own form of justice. It's likely he's the one who killed her and when his posse leader found out, he was executed for it."

"Case closed," Bolan said, unable to keep the sarcasm out of his voice.

Anders shrugged again. "It's where the trail leads," he said. "I've seen it before down here."

"It seems a little convenient to me," Bolan replied. "So if the killings here are personal, why take out a senator's daughter? Or is that coincidence?"

Anders shrugged and looked away. He looked back and Bolan knew that the next words out of his mouth were going to be a lie. He didn't care about territorial people, but liars who were supposed to be on his team were bothersome. Anders started to speak and Bolan held up his hand.

"Look, Anders, I don't know what crap you're getting ready to spout, but just...don't. If there is a link to the senator that you suspect, then you need to let me know. If not, you're likely to have a bad day. I don't care about political garbage, I care about getting the people who did this and seeing them brought to justice."

Anders took a step back and looked up at Bolan.

"No bullshit."

"No bullshit."

"All right, there are drugs and guns coming out of Jamaica, and we can't seem to stem the flow."

"What does that have to do with the senator?"

"Someone is helping them and I intend to find the culprit," Anders said.

"She was staying at the Goldshore Resort, according to what I've got on file."

"That's right," he said. "Are you going to check it out?"

"Yes," Bolan said. "There's something about all this that sets my teeth on edge."

"What aren't you telling me?" Anders asked. "If I knew more, maybe I could help more. You said no bullshit."

"Maybe so," Bolan said, standing up. "But if I told you, I'd have to kill you." He stared hard at the man. "We wouldn't want that, now, would we?"

"Funny," Anders said. "But you aren't the first CIA badass to try that with me. If you get serious, let me know if you want my help. Jamaica isn't like most playgrounds. The mix of serious thugs with tourists is a pressure cooker, and the locals have no problem sending a clear message that if they aren't left alone to do as they wish, they will seriously damage the notion of an ideal tourist spot. Other than that, there's nothing else I can offer you."

"I don't need anything else," he said. "I'll see myself out."

"Good," Anders said, not bothering to rise or offer to shake hands again. "And, Agent Cooper?"

Bolan stopped halfway to the door and turned back. "Yes?"

"Obeah may seem like superstitious nonsense, but it's

very real to the people who believe in it. I advise you to be careful. Lots of people just…disappear in Jamaica."

"I'm always careful, Mr. Anders," Bolan replied. "It's why I'm still alive and so many of my enemies aren't." He turned his back on the man and walked out the door.

Bolan parked his rental car across the street from the Goldshore Villas Resort. He knew from reading the dossier on Amber Carson that she'd been staying there, in her father's condominium, while in Jamaica. He'd taken the time to do some quick research, but the pictures he'd seen online hadn't done the place justice. It was a monument to wealth and excess, brought to life in the form of a private resort for the rich and powerful.

High adobe walls were decorated with vines and flowers, providing beauty, privacy and a botanical scene before a person even entered the front door. The main building was the largest of three, reaching up ten stories, with two smaller towers of eight stories on either side. The walls were nothing but windows—obviously opaque—to provide a view of the ocean and the beaches, or the island itself. A gated entrance protected a circular drive, and beyond it Bolan could see the double doors trimmed in polished brass. A valet and a bellman waited at a small podium.

He crossed the street and stopped at the inconspicuous, though obviously new, guard shack. Inside, a uniformed security officer stared back at him through the glass. "Can I help you, sir?"

Bolan showed him his CIA credentials. "I'm Special Agent Matt Cooper, CIA. I'd like to see the manager."

"Do you have an appointment, sir?"

"No, I don't," he replied. "Just call the desk and ask him if I can talk to him for a few minutes."

"You and every other guy with a badge wanting access," he said. "Hold on." He let go of the button that allowed them to converse through the small speaker in the glass and picked up a house phone inside the booth. He spoke a few words into the receiver, then hung the phone up.

"You can go on in," he said. "Sorry about making you wait."

Bolan lightly tapped the glass. "Better safe than sorry, right?" he asked.

"That's what they're saying now, since that girl got killed," the guard said. "Before, the gates were just for decoration. This booth is brand-new, and I was only hired a few days ago. They brought in a new security manager, too."

"I imagine things will settle down soon," Bolan said.

"I hope not," the man replied with a grin. "Easiest guard job I ever had catering to the rich folk. Not too many people want to make a fuss with the richies around. They want them to spend their money and then bring their friends to spend their money. Even the posses leave the tourists alone in this area."

Bolan walked over as the guard opened the pedestrian gate for him. He stepped through and followed the walk around the drive to the front door, where the bellman was waiting to open it. Bolan thanked him and moved forward into the lobby.

Plush carpeting in warm colors and leather furnishings greeted him, while indirect light kept the interior lit without being overly bright. The greenery from the outside continued throughout the lobby, creating a tropical paradise with hidden alcoves and paths that led out to the gardens. Quiet New Age music played on hidden speakers. The front desk was along the wall to his left and topped with a highly polished slab of driftwood large enough to serve as a raft should the need arise. An attractive young woman stood behind it, and she smiled when she saw him.

"Agent Cooper?" she asked. "Go right in. Mr. Kroger is waiting for you." She gestured at a door positioned to one side of the front desk.

"Thanks," he said, scanning the lobby for trouble even as he went to the door and opened it to see a large office dominated by a desk and multiple file cabinets. Behind the desk, a thin, tired-looking man waved him in.

"Please, Agent Cooper," he said, gesturing at one of the chairs, "have a seat." He rose and offered his hand. "John Kroger, by the way. I'm the general manager of the resort."

"I appreciate your taking the time to see me without an appointment," he said. "The guard out front made it clear that things have been hectic."

Kroger laughed dispiritedly. "It's been a trip through hell," he admitted. "Ever since Amber Carson was…found."

"She was raped and murdered," Bolan said bluntly. "There's no need to soft sell it with me."

Kroger shuddered. "I find it all so horrible," he said. "As I've told the other investigators, nothing like this has ever happened here."

"In Jamaica?" he asked.

"No, no," Kroger said. "I mean here at the resort. We're not that kind of place. Even during spring break, most of our younger guests are well-behaved." He stood up and paced back and forth behind his desk, waving his stick-figure arms. "I don't understand it," he continued. "Oh, they'll come here and drink, maybe get high, but they don't usually cause trouble for anyone but the housekeeping staff. Their families compensate the hotel well for any damages, and everyone continues to have a good time. It's a long-standing tradition down here. They come and play, spend lots of money and we don't ask a lot of questions. The parents like to send them here because they know our staff is discreet."

Bolan watched as the man finally stopped and sat once more. "It's not an easy situation for anyone," he said. "And I don't want to take up a lot of your time...."

"Of course, of course," Kroger said. "I apologize. I've talked to so many people this past week, and none of them have been able or willing to tell me anything. I don't even worry about what this will do to our business, you understand. I *know* Ms. Carson's father personally. How will I ever look him in the eye again?"

Bolan already knew that the senator's death was being kept quiet for a few days for security reasons, so telling Kroger anything about it now wouldn't serve any larger purpose. "I'm sure he'll understand that you weren't responsible," he said.

"I hope so, very much," he said. "Now, what can I do to help you?"

"Honestly, I'm not sure there's much you can do," he admitted. "At this point, I'm simply following my instincts. Would you mind if I took a look around the property, maybe talked to some of the staff?"

"Not at all," Kroger said. "I can escort you, if you like, or our new security manger, Mr. Kowal, whichever you prefer."

"I'd like to meet Mr. Kowal, anyway," Bolan said. "Since he's new, he may be able to offer a unique perspective."

Kroger agreed and picked up the phone, calling Mr. Kowal, who arrived several minutes later, and introduced himself. "Call me Rob," he said.

Kowal was a rather unassuming man, with brown hair and eyes that likely made him unnoticeable most of the time.

His manner was one of friendly professionalism. "What would you like to see first, Agent Cooper?"

"Let's start with the security tapes from the night Amber Carson was last seen alive," he suggested. "Then I'd like to talk with housekeeping."

"If you'll follow me?" he asked.

Bolan nodded, thanked Kroger and followed Kowal out of the office. The security manager's office was a short distance down a back hallway, and Bolan found himself pleasantly surprised. Most hotels and resorts couldn't afford—or wouldn't spend—the money for a genuine security professional, let alone the kinds of equipment on display here. The office was clean and well organized, and a bank of camera monitors was placed against one wall. They displayed views of every hallway, the lobby, the driveway and the back patio area. A uniformed security officer was watching the monitors closely, occasionally tapping a button to change a camera angle.

"Impressive," Bolan said. "This is a pretty nice setup for a resort."

"Unfortunately, it's not as good as it could be," Kowal said. "I was brought on board just a few days ago, and it's too late to help that young woman."

"What was the security situation when you were hired?" Bolan asked.

"Pretty standard," he said. "The cameras were all operational and recording, but there was no monitoring security staff. After midnight, the resort was running only a single security officer for the entire property, and he spent most of his nights rousting drunk rich kids instead of looking for real trouble."

"What have you changed since you came on board?"

Kowal gestured to the man seated at the monitors. "As you can see, I've got a man assigned just to watch the camera feeds—rotating staff there every three hours to keep their eyes fresh. I also added the gate guard, and we have four officers on foot patrol during the day–it bumps to six between 6:00 p.m. and midnight, and then drops to three between midnight and 4:00 a.m."

"Sounds about right," Bolan said. "Any trouble so far?"

The security manager shook his head in disgust. "Nothing out of the ordinary. Drunk rich kids carrying on, for the most part. A couple of minor scuffles out on the patio, and once on the beach—all easily handled and nothing out of the ordinary."

"Have you talked to the staff on duty that night?" he asked. "Reviewed the video footage?"

"Both," Kowal said. He turned to the officer seated at the monitors. "Dave, can you bring up the footage from the night of Amber Carson's murder, please? Just from the patio." He moved to a blank monitor, turned it on and gestured for Bolan to sit down.

Both men watched as Amber and her friends drank shots out on the patio, then saw her move to get something to eat. There wasn't an audio feed. "Who's the guy hitting on her?" Bolan asked.

"Actually, a member of the staff. He was off duty, and so long as things didn't get out of line, the management had allowed it. I've since changed that policy."

"Wise," he said. "Has this employee been questioned?"

"By the local police, myself, Mr. Kroger and two federal law-enforcement officers who came in yesterday evening," Kowal said.

Bolan thought that was curious. He asked which agency the federal officers were with, and Kowal snorted. "They showed FBI credentials, but I don't think so. Maybe military or NSA, but not FBI."

"What makes you say that?"

"Educated guess," Kowal said. "They didn't talk like FBI."

"You seem to know your way around law enforcement," Bolan said. "Better than most resort security officers I've ever heard of. What's your background?"

Kowal smiled. "Secret Service until four years ago. I quit to launch my own company."

"Doing resort security? Kind of a step down, if you don't mind my saying so."

This time Kowal actually laughed. "No, my company is a security consulting agency. Once they're set up here and I've got a good man in place to run things, I'll be on my way to wherever the next job takes me. It may not sound as cool as Secret Service, but it's about ten times the money."

"Makes sense," Bolan said. "So, what's your take on this situation?"

"Jamaica is a gilt-covered cesspit," he said. "But generally speaking, the real bad guys, the posse crews, leave the tourists alone. Too much trouble—high risk, low reward. I think Amber Carson was targeted, if what I've heard is true."

"What have you heard?" he asked.

"She was raped, ritualistically murdered, and then somehow her body was rigged with a light explosive that was attached to weaponized anthrax. When it went off, it killed Senator Carson, some folks in the examination room where they were conducting the autopsy, and turned Bethesda Naval Hospital into a quarantine zone."

Bolan leaned back in his chair and reassessed the man sitting before him. Not only was his information dead-on accurate, but it was only known to a handful of people in the world right now. "I thought you were out of the Secret Service," he finally said.

"I am," Kowal said. "But I still have friends there, and I like to keep in the loop about what's going on in that end of things. You know how it is. You're never really out of service."

"You're well-informed," he admitted. "Most of that hasn't been made public yet. Kroger still thinks her father is alive. Have you heard anything from the staff that makes you think they might know more than they ought to?"

"No, but I'm the new guy and not a local, so that makes me persona non grata with the islanders. It's a closed community in general and really hard to break into, but I'm not here to make best friends. I'm here to get a job done."

"Kroger's going to find out, probably sooner than later. They won't be able to keep that under wraps for long," Bolan said.

"I know," he said. "But he won't find out from me. Right now, I'm just doing the job I was hired to do—make the resort as secure as possible. Though that horse has already left the barn, I think."

"Me, too," Bolan said. "I just wish I knew where the damn thing ran off to."

After finishing up with the security manager, Bolan decided to give the property a quick visual inspection. Kowal had happily agreed. Though the man seemed more than competent, another set of eyes might spot something new or different. First, Bolan went up to Amber's floor and checked out the condominium, which was still protected by police tape and unchanged from the night of her death. Then, he went all the way to the roof, which turned out to be unremarkable—as did the beach, the patio and the walkways around the main resort building. In short, nothing jumped out at him as out of place.

Walking along the rear of the building, Bolan heard two male voices on the other side of a brick screening wall, and he stopped to listen. The conversation was unclear, but both men seemed to be unhappy with their jobs. He started to dismiss them and move on, when they walked away from the area with their backs to him. One of the men wore a sleeveless T-shirt, and it revealed a heavily inked tattoo that looked all too familiar—the symbol of the Undead Posse.

Pausing to take another look, Bolan saw that the other man sported the same tattoo. Two people from the Undead

Posse working here felt like a lot more than a coincidence to him. Bolan decided to follow them to see if they led him somewhere interesting—or at least somewhere he might be able to ask them some questions in a more private setting.

Bolan followed the two men as they left the employee's entrance and exit area and walked toward a private parking lot shielded from sight by a row of massive palm trees and a vine-covered iron fence. They rounded the corner and Bolan walked a bit faster, not wanting to lose them. As he came around the fence, he saw that they had paused, and one had drawn a compact semiautomatic handgun.

Bolan hit the ground in a dive roll just as the shot rang out. He didn't stop his movement, just kept the roll moving forward until he found his feet, then launched himself full force into the man with the handgun, driving his head like a battering ram into his gut and knocking him to the ground.

The man lost his grip on the gun, which bounced and clattered over the pavement of the parking lot. Out of the corner of his eye, Bolan saw the second man take off running. He'd have to finish this one quickly if he had any hope at all of catching up. He drove his knee piston-style into the crotch of the man beneath him, then shifted as the man groaned in pain and dropped the knee into his rib cage. Bolan felt at least one give way beneath his weight, and the groan became a breathy scream.

"Who are you?" Bolan demanded, leaning back slightly to let the man breathe.

Through a grimace of pain, the man said, "Death!" He spit the word as he brought around a hidden knife with his free hand, trying to stab the blade into Bolan's neck.

The Executioner grabbed his wrist before he could connect, silently thanking his lucky stars that he'd seen it coming, and twisted the joint. As the man fought beneath him, Bolan contorted the wrist further, the ligaments snapping as he pushed it down, down, and then with a final shove stuck the blade into the man's throat. The nameless thug twitched beneath him, then sagged in the release of death.

"Damn it," he muttered, pushing himself up off the body that lay on the ground. He looked around for the other man, and saw him slipping into a Jeep on the far side of the parking lot. Knowing he had no time, Bolan leaped to his feet and took off running back toward the resort and the street where he'd parked his rental car. He ran all out, shouting for the guard to open the pedestrian gate.

The man came out looking stunned at Bolan's sudden appearance.

"Open it!" Bolan yelled as he slammed into the gate. "Open it now!"

The guard hurried into his shack, and the big American saw the Jeep pull out of the employee lot two blocks down. The gate buzzed and Bolan shoved himself through it.

"What's going—" the guard tried to say as he ran past.

Bolan didn't have time for conversation. He raced to his car and jumped in, gunned the engine and took off after the Jeep.

The roads were crowded enough that he had to weave through traffic like a madman. Tires squealed and horns honked as he forced his vehicle past irritated drivers until he saw the Jeep ahead of him by several blocks and he felt comfortable enough to slow down. The traffic thinned as the Jeep headed out of Montego Bay, back toward Kingston. He stayed back as far as he could, noting how the driver of the Jeep was moving along the street carelessly and dangerously. It careened around cars that were moving slower than he wanted to go, and a couple of times he nearly caused an accident. Still, Bolan didn't think the man could see that he was being followed so much as he was in a hurry to get away.

The Jeep continued on down the highway, and Bolan

was thankful that this was really the only road between the two cities. A number of vehicles stayed on the highway the whole time, so there was no reason for the driver of the Jeep to think he was being followed simply because Bolan's car happened to be behind him. It took a couple of hours for them to reach Kingston, and then he had no choice but to move closer.

The late-afternoon traffic was getting heavier and heavier, and if Bolan lost his mark, then all of this would have been for nothing. The soldier wished he hadn't had to kill the man back at the resort. No doubt that Kowal and Kroger would be upset by another death on the property—even a necessary one.

The heart of Kingston was the polar opposite of Montego Bay, which was mostly a tourist area. Kept clean and inviting, with signs of wealth the hallmark of the coastal area, Montego Bay was welcoming and looked safe. The heart of Kingston was anything but hospitable: it was a place for the locals, mostly members of Jamaican posses. Spray-painted graffiti, rusted or burned-out cars and garbage in the streets made for a stunning contrast to where he'd just come from.

As the Jeep got closer to the Tivoli Gardens district, Bolan began to wish he was in an armored truck, instead of a four-door rental car that wouldn't hold off a determined attack by a Chihuahua, let alone a gang of Jamaican thugs.

The fighting in the Tivoli Gardens area was practically legend, and the area had been highlighted in his mission briefing materials as extremely dangerous to outsiders. He knew that already. One large graffiti sign said Shoes of Jamaica and had an arrow pointing to a bloody shoe on the ground.

Bolan maneuvered his car through large stacks of pallets, and vehicles that were parked partly in the road. He was making another turn when the Jeep stopped and cars swarmed from different directions to pin his vehicle between them. Two cars were behind him, the Jeep in front and another blocked the exit to his right as several Jamaicans got out of their cars and began to move in on his rental. Two men were holding crowbars, while a third held a bat with massive nails through the end.

"Here we go," Bolan muttered, watching in his mirror as the closer of them reached the back of his car. He slammed the stick into Reverse and gunned the engine. The tires screeched and the man tried to get out of the way, but he wasn't fast enough. The rear bumper crunched into his legs, and he let out a scream of agony even as he smashed the crowbar he was carrying into the back windshield. The glass spidered but somehow held.

Bolan shifted into First and floored the gas pedal, ramming into the back end of the Jeep and narrowly missing the man he'd been following, who'd gotten out and was approaching his car with the others. The Jeep shuddered with the impact and rolled forward slightly, offering a narrow exit. The sudden burst of gunfire from behind made it more than clear to Bolan that it was time to go. But first it seemed as if making a point was necessary.

The Executioner drew his Desert Eagle, aimed through the passenger window and fired. The .50-caliber round shattered the safety glass with ease and made a mess of the nearest posse member. The entrance wound was bad, but the exit wound was worse, and the velocity knocked the man backward into the vehicle he'd been driving, a bloody, dying heap.

Another burst of gunfire blew out Bolan's back window, and he ducked lower, shoved the car into gear and aimed for the small opening. His car clipped the Jeep with the grating sound of metal, but he managed to make it through. Behind him, angry shouts and gunshots continued, and he knew they'd follow. Considering his mode of transportation, Bolan considered himself extremely lucky to have all four tires and a vehicle that ran at all.

The other vehicles were behind him in seconds, still shooting. Bolan whipped around a corner and found himself in a narrow lane that was crowded with wooden pallets and ended in a rusted chain-link fence. With the other cars right behind him, he didn't have any other choices but to floor the accelerator, shift and plow straight ahead. The pallets shattered with a crash and wooden splinters flew in all directions. He ducked again as he hit the fence, which gave way before him, but not before a large section of it smashed into his windshield, spidering the glass.

Obviously, the people living in the area were not unaccustomed to gunfire. Whereas most people would stay hidden, Bolan saw these residents running out of their homes to see what was going on. He yanked hard on the steering wheel, choosing the first street that went away from the residential buildings.

Just as he glanced in the mirror, a burst of automatic gunfire sounded and took out the last of his rear windshield. Bullets pounded into the heavy cloth seats. Bolan accelerated until he saw a large truck blocking the road in front of him. "Damn it," he said, tapping the brakes and looking for a way to pass. Knowing it was a risk, he started to move around, but another barrage of gunfire took out the back tires of the truck and the sudden change in speeds forced them together. Metal crunched, and Bolan slammed on the brakes, letting the truck go past, then he downshifted, popped the clutch and moved to the other side of the truck, which was weaving all over the road.

He steered around another corner, only to see an oncoming pickup truck headed straight for him. In the bed, two men opened fire with mini-MAC-10s. "Son of a—" he said as two trails of bullets ran up the length of his hood. Bolan ducked, then popped back up, the Desert Eagle in hand. He fired off five quick shots, and the final one smashed the engine block of the truck. Smoke rolled as it skidded to a halt.

Bolan rocketed past the slowing vehicle and slammed on his brakes as he realized he was at a dead end. He locked the car into Reverse, spinning it and spearheading his way back into the oncoming cars. The slam from the side caught Bolan by surprise and knocked his car into an apartment building.

Gunfire poured in through the windows as Bolan shoved the driver's seat backward and shimmied into the rear area. He opened the pass-through compartment, pulled out his briefcase and opened it in one smooth motion. The gunfire suddenly stopped, and he could hear a voice shouting, "Enough! Enough! Stop!"

Pulling two grenades out of the case, he pulled the pins and waited three seconds. Then he popped through the sunroof like a paramilitary jack-in-the-box and tossed the bombs directly at the feet of the men closing in on his vehicle. They detonated milliseconds after impact, and the explosions ripped through the gang. Screams sounded as shrapnel tore into their bodies.

Bolan grabbed the case in one hand as he bailed out of the car. It contained his primary arsenal and there was no way he was leaving it behind.

He whipped around the corner and into an alley as the first rounds of renewed gunfire sounded behind him. Using the building as cover, he put the case on the ground and rapidly assembled the Tavor MTAR-21 mini assault rifle inside it. Slamming the magazine home, he risked a quick look around the corner.

They were headed his way once more.

"Persistent," Bolan muttered, glancing down the alleyway. He needed to either end this or escape—and fast. The risks to his mission were mounting quickly. He couldn't do the job if he was seriously injured, killed or captured, but these men obviously didn't care about civilian casualties, either. They were in an area of rundown apartment buildings and a few shops. With all the gunfire, sooner or later there were going to be people hurt or dead who had nothing to do with the situation.

He risked another look and opened up with the Tavor in short, sharp bursts. The building facades echoed with the sound, and two of the approaching posse members went down before the others found cover.

Jacob Crisp stared out the window at the small market that filled the streets below his window. He smiled as the armored police vehicles drove by and bystanders threw rotted fruits and vegetables at the intruding vehicles. The irony that they were protesting in small ways because of his supposed death and all of the things that his posse had created was not lost on him. The vehicles continued out of the square, and Jacob closed the wooden shutter, blocking out further opportunity for distraction, and returned his attention to the men behind him.

Bastiene Durene was his most loyal companion. At six foot he was a couple of inches taller than Crisp, but leaner and meaner. Everyone called him Spook because he seemed to appear and disappear without any evidence. It made him an effective killer and an even more effective spy. He had almost left Spook out of his reincarnation, but he knew that the man would find out eventually anyway and then only see the slight as a betrayal.

The other man was a newly hired gun, Christofer Denham, a drug smuggler with the right connections whom he had done some time with. He had also built up a lot of trust with the senator's daughter and knew just the right channels to get anything, anytime, anywhere.

"I don't like this, man," Spook said.

"You sound like an old mother hen, my man. What is your concern? We've dealt with the authorities before," Crisp said.

"Not like this. The stakes have never been so high."

"You knew they'd turn up the heat," Denham snapped. "What did you expect? That they'd not send every hired gun in the States down here looking?

"This is exactly what we want, and we want to keep them looking here. We want to keep them looking in the places that don't matter anymore. Every time they get close, they will find that the trail of bodies is the only thing that will keep them company. This man…this Cooper, he will be the same as all the others—dead. Is everything set up at the cemetery?" Crisp asked.

"Yeah, they'll be ready with what we need. Do you have everything you'll need?" Spook asked Denham.

"All set. This should be even more satisfying than the girl."

"The Obeah man has to do his ceremony. You'll give him what he needs for later?"

"It'll all be set. Just make sure my payment is ready before I get there, or the only thing leaking from those bodies will be rotting flesh."

ANDERS PACED in his office, waiting for the phone call. He picked up a file from the desk and absently flipped through it, trying anything to relieve the tension that was starting to build. The intensity of the whole operation had increased dramatically with the death of the senator. The daughter would have been enough to get the point across, but killing the senator was putting everything in jeopardy.

The phone rang and he paused in midstep. It rang again,

snapping him out of his contemplation. He flipped the cover of the folder closed and dropped it onto the desk as he picked up the phone.

"Anders."

"I got your message. What's so damn urgent?"

"I've had every damn agency you can name down here, including the CIA. You didn't tell me to expect a spook."

"If I were you, I wouldn't be surprised at a visit from Jesus H. Christ himself. The White House is telling everyone that getting to those responsible is a high-level priority, and there's a lot of pressure for an immediate or sooner resolution."

Anders sighed. "You've got to slow things down up there. This whole thing is going to spin out of control at this rate. We can't keep all of this in order and not expect the heat to fall on us," he said.

"You need to relax. None of this is unexpected. Of course they're going to investigate. We *want* them to, remember? As long as you do your job, all roads are going to lead to the Undead Posse. There is nothing that connects us to those morons, plus they are happy to take the glory."

"And the casualties?" Anders asked. "There's going to be more casualties. Maybe a lot more before this is over."

"The posse can damn well take those, too," he said. "It's one of the better reasons to use them."

BOLAN DUCKED behind an old abandoned Buick that had two flat tires on one side. He reloaded, quietly chambering the next round and then checking how much ammo he had left. With only two spare magazines for the Tavor and one more for his Desert Eagle, he was going to have to get out of there fast. He didn't have the ammo for a sustained firefight.

He scanned the alley behind him. Aside from the piles of trash and a rusted-out garbage bin, he didn't see much in the way of an escape route. At the end of the alley, he could hear the shouts of the posse members as they debated who was going in after him. Popping up over the trunk of the Buick, he fired another short burst from the Tavor, sending everyone back into cover. “Damn,” he said.

The light tap on his shoulder caused him to spin and nearly pull the trigger on a kid that couldn’t have been more than twelve. “Hey, mister,” he whispered. He grinned at Bolan.

“Kid, you better get out of here now,” Bolan said. “You’re going to get hurt.”

The boy smiled and asked, “You want to get out of here?”

Bolan quickly reassessed. “Where? How?”

“How much?” the kid asked.

“Fifty,” Bolan said.

The kid shook his head. “A hundred.”

“Done,” he said. “When we’re clear.”

“Then let’s go,” he said, gesturing back into the alley. “Before more of them come.”

Bolan popped up once more over the car and fired a two-second burst, then turned and followed the boy who wove his way past garbage bins and piles of trash as if he knew the path by heart. He bounded past a stack of moldy mattresses, then turned and gestured toward a crack in the brick wall of the building. “There,” he said.

“It’s a crack in the wall,” Bolan replied, taking a quick glance behind them. “Neither one of us will fit.”

“That’s the idea,” the kid said, then leaned forward and pushed.

Bolan watched in amazement as the wall slid backward, revealing a dark opening beyond.

“Inside,” the boy said. “Hurry.”

THE BOY COULD ALMOST stand as they moved through the tunnel, but the fit was a little tighter for Bolan. They reached the end of the passageway and came out almost a block from where they began. Seeing no signs of followers, Bolan holstered his pistol before stepping out onto the street and following the boy into a café.

The little shop was literally a hole in the wall, barely bigger than the hidden tunnel they'd used to get there. The building was one of the many casualties of the constant fighting between the posses and the government. The front stone entrance that had once held double doors now stood open, and the tables were visible to any passerby. The roof remained intact, and the owner had placed several tropical plants to soften the jagged stone edges. There was no remnant of rubble or debris, and it was clear that the damage had been done for some time. Apparently the owner had no intention of re-creating the closed front in the immediate future.

Bolan walked in, noticed the menu written on a chalkboard and sat at the first available table. He glanced around as he ran through his options. Getting shot at and running for his life was not something new to him, but the lack of leads was troubling. He considered going back to the embassy for more information, but his gut said that everything there was not as it should be and someone had told the posse he was coming.

The boy, who'd told Bolan to sit down, then disappeared. When he returned he waltzed up to Bolan's table with a pitcher of water in his hand.

"What can I get ya?"

"You can start with some answers," Bolan said. "Now you're a waiter? Ten minutes ago, you were my rescuer."

"I do what makes money," he said, shrugging. Then he looked emphatically at Bolan. "And you owe me some."

"So I do," he said, pulling out his wallet. He removed a hundred-dollar bill and handed it to the kid. "That makes us square," he said. "Unless you want to earn more."

"I always want to earn more," the boy replied. "You think I want to live here forever?"

"All right, then I'll take today's special—the goat—and some information."

"The special is ten dollars," he said, "but information will cost you more."

"I can pay," he said. "But not until I know if what you can tell me is worth anything."

"Mister, there are two kinds of guys that come here, ones from here and ones looking for someone from here. No one says they want information if they are looking for the best fishing spot, eh?"

"I'd say you're right, but that still doesn't tell me if any information you have might be useful."

"I saved your life, didn't I?"

Bolan smiled. "Maybe," he said. "It was getting tight back there. Food first, then information. We'll see what it's worth after you talk."

The kid shrugged and started to turn back to the kitchen, which Bolan assumed was on the other side of the wall… somewhere. When dining local, he'd long since learned it was better to eat and not ask too many questions.

"Hey, kid, what's your name?" he asked.

"Reggie Dequain."

"All right, Reggie. It's good to meet you. I'm Matt."

"I'll get your food, Matt," he said, then skipped away.

Bolan drained a glass of water, refilled it from the pitcher the boy had left on the table and waited. Several minutes passed before Reggie returned, bearing a large plate in one hand. He set it on the table and produced some silverware wrapped in a paper napkin. The food smelled good.

The curry goat was served over a large bed of rice, and fried plantains were stacked to one side. Bolan removed the silverware from the napkin and dug in, grinning at the boy as the mild spices hit his stomach. The soldier ate quickly and in silence, finishing it all, knowing that he might not get another chance to eat for hours.

Reggie was unusually patient for a kid and kept his silence while Bolan ate. When he'd finished and put his napkin on the empty plate, Reggie picked it up and put it in a bus tub on the other side of the room. Then he returned and sat back down.

"Okay, Reggie, let's talk."

"What do you want to know?" he asked.

"I want to know about the Undead Posse," Bolan said. "Everything you know and anything you've heard."

"Mister, that's gonna be big expensive."

"Name your price," he said.

"Ten thousand dollars," Reggie said, not even pausing.

"Good knowing you, kid," he said. "Thanks for the food." He took a ten-dollar bill out of his wallet and put it on the table. "That ought to cover lunch."

"How about five thousand?"

"You have cable television, Reggie?" Bolan asked. "You must, because you sound like you've been watching too many movies. No deal. Have a nice day." He stood up, pushing his chair away from the table.

"Okay, okay," Reggie said. "How about another hundred? With what you gave me earlier, I can finish paying the rent."

Disgusted that a kid would have to be in that position, but knowing that by comparison with much he had seen, the boy had it easier than many, he nodded. "That I can do."

Bolan pulled the money out of his wallet and passed it over to him.

"Now, tell me what you know about the Undead Posse."

"The one's chasing you? Bad mojo," he said. "Double bad."

Reggie jumped up from the table and made a run for the exit, but Bolan anticipated the move and grabbed him as he went by.

"Hey, let me go!"

"So this is the information that a hundred dollars gets me?"

"On the Undead Posse, yeah, that's all you get. No one talks to the cops about the Undead unless they want to be… you know…*the* dead."

"Look, kid, I'm not the cops. You helped me out with them back there, right?"

"That was easy," he said. "They couldn't see me!"

"I'm just trying to figure out some stuff," Bolan said. "If you help me, I'll double that hundred I just gave you."

Reggie was looking hard enough at his shoes that Bolan thought they might turn into Hermes sandals and fly him out of his current predicament. He held on to the boy tighter. Reggie looked up and stared into his eyes. Bolan could see the trace amounts of fear and confusion. The soldier reached into his pocket and pulled out the next hundred.

"Here, you take the money. We sit. We talk. If you don't like where the conversation goes we stop talking and you take the money and go on your way. Deal?"

Reggie waited another minute. He reached out to take the money. Bolan pulled his hand away and raised an eyebrow.

"Okay," the kid said.

Bolan handed him the money and waved Reggie back to his chair. Bolan took his seat at the table.

"Now, there are posses all over the place around here, and most like to hear their exploits shouted to the rafters. What makes the Undead Posse different?"

"They aren't like the others."

"How?'

"They have magic."

"Magic?'

"You don't believe me. You're an American, you don't believe in anything."

"I didn't say I don't believe you, I just want to understand."

"You believe in magic?" Reggie asked.

"I've seen a lot of things, especially here in Jamaica. Some can't be explained very easily. I don't know if it's magic, but I'm willing to look at all the possibilities."

Reggie looked at him and smiled.

"You're different."

"I'm something all right. Tell me about the magic."

"They perform dark rituals in the May Pen cemetery. The spirits there are restless. They make them do things."

"What kinds of things?"

Before he could answer, an old woman came out of the back. "Don't you be talkin' 'bout that stuff, boy! You know better!"

Reggie rolled his eyes at Bolan. "It's just talk, Gram," he said. "Besides, he's payin'!"

"It don't matter what he pays. If he keeps diggin' around, the Spook will get him." She shook a dried-up old chicken foot in Bolan's direction to emphasize her point.

"The Spook?" he asked.

"He ain't real," Reggie said. "At least, I don't think so. He runs with the Undead Posse."

Before he could continue, the boy stood up and guided the old woman back into the kitchen. Under his breath, Bolan heard him talk about the rent money and the woman muttering about curses.

When he returned, Bolan said, "You were telling me about the posse's magic?"

"They made that girl kill her father."

"How do you know about that?"

"The stories started after she died. The streets said that they put a spirit inside her and that she would kill him. They used her to kill her own family."

Reggie looked down into his cup. His hands trembled and

Bolan waited for him to say more, but after a few minutes he knew he wouldn't.

"Reggie, one more question, and you can go."

"What?"

"Where is the cemetery?"

The sun was disappearing into the water as Bolan approached the exterior gate of the May Pen Cemetery. A Kingston landmark, the cemetery was undergoing renovations, but much of it was still a mess from the storms that were prevalent in the area. Overgrown plants and vines, exposed wooden coffins stacked in random piles, even the occasional bone was sticking out of the ground. Some of the paths were clear and lined with fresh-cut flowers, while others were all but invisible. Slipping inside, Bolan crouched behind a large tombstone and watched as the lights of the chapel were extinguished and a priest stepped outside.

Two armed men stood on either side of the chapel entrance, the Undead Posse tattoo emblazoned on their arms. The priest passed them, keeping his eyes on the ground and making the sign of the cross. He was muttering, but Bolan could only pick out a few words that were tinged with fear. The priest rounded the corner and left the cemetery.

Bolan moved through the overgrowth and worked his way to the opposite side of the building. He hid once more and waited for the sentry to make the edge of the building. Pulling a long, thin wire from beneath his belt, Bolan watched as the guard moved forward then turned to make his next pass. The Executioner rose silently to his feet behind him, looping the wire around the man's throat in a blur and driving his knee into the center of the man's back. With no oxygen, their struggle was silent and short. Bolan used the thug's own weight to finish the job.

The other sentry rounded the corner as his partner was being lowered to the ground. Before he could get off a warning, Bolan pulled a small throwing blade from his boot and whipped it toward the man in one smooth motion. The knife slid easily into the man's throat, cutting off his shout before it was more than a soft whistling sound in the air.

Bolan quickly dragged both of the bodies to the back side of the chapel. Using his handheld computer, he snapped a picture of each man's face and did a thumbprint scan as well, then sent the information over a virtual private network—to Stony Man Farm. At this point, any information he might be able to pick up could be valuable. Nothing in this mission felt right, and so far his best informant was a twelve-year-old kid.

On the move once more, Bolan chose to take up a position inside the old clock tower. A three-story stone structure, it would provide plenty of cover. The entrances and windows were boarded up, and it took a bit of time to find a board loose enough for him to wiggle free quietly. Once that was done, he slipped inside, replacing the board behind him.

The clock mechanism was no longer functioning, and the wooden stairs to the upper levels appeared to be less than sturdy. Bolan leaned against the wall and waited. Running his hand along the interior stone walls didn't reveal very much about his surroundings. On the outside, he'd noted that the tower was light browns, oranges and white. The little bit of remaining light that seeped through the boards showed parts of the wall blackened from a fire, while the rest was a chalky white stone.

The time ticked by slowly, and the night sky finally appeared. Shortly after, Bolan heard footfalls where the path turned from the soft soil to rock. The distant sound of car doors closing, and more footsteps on the path told him that even more members of the Undead Posse were arriving. He sat and listened, occasionally spying out the spaces in the boarded-up window as the members of the posse took up positions around a fresh grave.

Bolan pulled out his night-vision goggles and slipped them on to get a better view of the grave they were apparently desecrating. The freshly chiseled name read Christian Ross, then beneath that, Beloved Son, followed by the dates of his birth and death. The boy had only been a teenager when he'd died less than a month ago.

Bolan pulled out his handheld computer and typed in the information. He ducked as he read the screen, not wanting the small glow from the device to give him away. The boy was the son of the Kingston chief of police, who'd been trying to rein in the posses for months. According to a newspaper account, the boy had died of complications from a virus. Bolan typed out a quick message to Aaron Kurtzman, Stony Man Farm's computer expert, asking him to get the boy's hospital records and then send them to him.

The posse had lit the area with torches, so Bolan put away the night-vision goggles and turned his attention back to the grave robbers. There were between ten and fifteen men total, and most were heavily armed. Those who weren't digging moved around the perimeter with military precision. The grave was less than a month old, and while the ground had settled some, the diggers made quick work of unearthing the casket. Using the ropes that had been used to lower the coffin into the ground, they lifted it up and placed it none-too-gently on the surface. The flames from the torches glinted off the polished wood and bronze handles. Three men who had been standing in the shadows moved into the light. Bolan was stunned to see that one of them was Jacob Crisp, a supposedly dead man he'd read about in his research before coming to Jamaica. He'd been running one of the big drug posses in the States and done eight years in prison before returning to the island. Later he'd been reported as dead. To his right was a well-armed man, a bodyguard of some kind, and on his left, a man dressed in robes with streaks of paint whorled on his face in various patterns. This had to be their voodoo priest, called an Obeah man. He was quietly chanting in a slow rhythm.

The group gathered around the casket, and two men on either ends pried open the lid. The group took a collective step back when the lid was opened. The Obeah man moved forward chanting louder. He took a pouch and sprinkled something on the body. Bolan couldn't see what they were doing, but the Obeah man moved around the coffin as he chanted. He nodded to two men who pulled the body from the coffin.

Bolan watched as they stumbled while trying to maneuver the awkward weight around the coffin and the gaping hole of the grave. They placed the body on a tarp on the ground. The Obeah man moved around it, chanting faster, as the body was positioned on the tarp. Bolan noticed that the two men who had moved the body wore surgical gowns and gloves.

The Obeah man held a knife in the air. He began to wave it, chanting as he went, and then knelt next to the body. He cut through the clothes and made an incision along the boy's arm. He moved to the ground in front of the grave and traced the same design in the dirt. They wrapped the body in the tarp and then took off their outer garments, throwing them into the coffin. The Obeah man lifted a gas can and poured it into the coffin and shouted.

"Let the dead rise. Let the son visit the sins on the father."

He struck a match and dropped it into the coffin, which

ignited, sending flames into the night air. Bolan stepped back into his hiding space as the flames illuminated the darkest corners and tried not to cough as the breeze carried the black smoke across the cemetery.

The men began to disperse except for the two who had exhumed the boy, Crisp and his bodyguard, and the Obeah man. The two body snatchers left briefly, then pulled up with a van and dragged the body into the back.

Bolan waited until the other men followed and then headed for his car. Before starting the engine, he pulled out his handheld computer and activated the GPS. His one experience driving here had proved to him that there were hundreds of alleys and unmarked streets, so tracking himself was his best bet at finding his way back if he ended up getting off the beaten path. For the moment, the van seemed to be following major streets.

For the better part of a half hour, the van moved away from the cemetery and into a more residential area. Houses sat behind high walls and strong gates, and the streetlamps in this part of town seemed to be on more than they were off. Suddenly, the van came to a halt in front of a large residence, and Bolan had to come to a fast stop himself and park. He was almost a full block away, but figuring out the address was simple enough. He typed in a search on the residence and realized that they were sitting in front of the home of the boy's father. There was no way that whatever was about to happen would be a good thing.

Remembering what the Obeah man had said during the ceremony, his heart lurched in his chest. Over the years, Bolan had too often seen the grief felt by a parent who had lost a child. In his experience, there was no torture that could cause more anguish. Between this man's duties as a police chief in an incredibly difficult area and the loss of his son, there was no doubt that the poor man had more than enough to handle without this. And as far as Bolan could tell, he actually wanted the law to prevail in the area.

Bolan watched as they dumped the body at the front gate and drove off. Torn between following them and preventing whatever catastrophe they had planned for the family, he hesitated briefly, then got out of the car and headed for the gate. His mind raced, thinking about the triggering mechanism that they had used on Amber Carson and wondering if they had something just as heinous planned for this family. The easiest way to continue to run the streets was to incapacitate anyone who gave a damn and put the fear of God into anyone who considered taking his or her place.

Bolan ran for the body, but tried to maintain some distance from the walls of the residence, which were likely protected by security cameras. Either way, he needed to get a perimeter set up around the body in case this was another anthrax attack. The lights on the main house came to life and dogs began to bark. Flood lamps along the top of the wall burst into brilliant white light as two men came running from the main house with guns drawn.

Bolan tried to shout a warning, but nothing could be heard over the chaos. He stopped as one man reached him and the other paused next to the body wrapped in the tarp.

"Stop. It could kill you!" Bolan yelled. "That could be a trap!"

"What is this?" a deep, tired voice asked.

Bolan knew without looking or asking that this was the boy's father. A quick look showed him a man in a police uniform, though the collar was undone. Dark circles made his already deep brown eyes appear almost black, and his hair was peppered, with short, gray curls. And if he needed further proof, the howl of pain when the guard moved the tarp away from the boy's face would have been all of the evidence he needed.

He looked up at the man, who had his weapon pointed at him.

"I was trying to stop them," Bolan said, raising his hands in a gesture of surrender. He wanted to tell them about the Undead Posse and added, "It was—" But then a heavy club came down on the back of his head and the flood lamps along the wall went as dark as his consciousness.

The harsh, blaring ring of a nearby phone echoed off the walls and penetrated Bolan's skull like a pneumatic drill. He rolled to his side and barely caught himself before hitting the concrete of the cell floor, while doing his best to stifle a groan of pain. He went back to his previous position and gingerly probed his skull for the lump he knew he'd find there. Sure enough, he had a good-size goose egg on the back of his head, and the scalp had split open, too. His hair was still sticky and matted with blood.

Bolan slowly sat up to explore his surroundings, but he knew from experience that jail cells were pretty much the same all over the world. Small, cramped and uncomfortable. This one was built of concrete blocks that had been painted over with a shade of lime green, where it hadn't been chipped away or written on. The cot he occupied was bare of any blanket or pillow, and the air smelled of the famously bad combination of vomit, urine and bleach. The walls echoed almost every little sound, making him feel as if he was underwater.

He rubbed the back of his head once more, then slowly got to his feet, trying to keep the world from spinning away from him. He eased over to the bars and leaned against them, inwardly cringing at the thought of what he was about to do to himself. Before he could talk himself out of it, he took a deep breath and shouted, "Guard!"

The pain that threatened to split his head in two was instantaneous. The world started to go black, and stars swam in front of his eyes. Gritting his teeth, Bolan waited for his vision to return. He held on to the bars and tried to convince his stomach that puking would only make his head want to explode again.

He didn't have to wait long for his request to be acted upon. The officer came to the bars.

"I need to talk to Ross," Bolan said.

The man raked the end of a flashlight across the bars as he paced in front of Bolan. The echoing clangs were like being trapped in a bell tower.

"He doesn't want to talk to you."

"It's a matter of life and death."

"His son is already dead and you dug up his body and dumped it on his front porch. Do you really think he is going to listen to anything that you have to say?"

He shoved the flashlight through the bars and jabbed Bolan in the ribs to accent his point.

"Look, I didn't dig up his son, but I saw the people who did, and what they did to him in the cemetery. They were wearing surgical masks and gloves."

"And why is that, do you think?"

"I think they were using the boy's body to deliver some kind of threat to Ross, maybe a virus or something."

"You are only saying that to make me think that you have something contagious as a way to get out of this jail," he said, jabbing the light into his ribs again.

"I never got near the body," Bolan said.

The guard laughed deeply. "Oh, you may not have started out near him, but they put you in the back of a truck with the body to bring you to the jail. You two were practically sharing a blanket when they brought you in."

"Perfect," Bolan muttered, trying to think past the pounding in his skull.

"Now you listen, man. That boy was a good boy and he didn't deserve to die, and he didn't deserve to be dug up by a dog like you."

"I know, but I didn't dig him up. That was the Undead Posse," Bolan said.

"Maybe so, but you are the one we caught. Your embassy has been notified of your arrest. If you are lucky, they will begin negotiations for your extradition back to America." The guard looked as if he wanted to jab him one final time, but instead spit on the floor at Bolan's feet, then turned and walked away.

Bolan tried to recall anything from his memory that might help jar what happened after he was hit. He remembered the hit, and there was only a small blur of a man kneeling next to the boy's body before the whole world went black. He was certain that there had to have been something wrong with the kid's body with the precautions that they were taking. He didn't know much about Obeah, but the surgical masks and gloves were a sign that something wasn't right. He couldn't imagine that members of the Undead Posse would be squeamish when it came to a body, so the gear meant something.

Bolan reached for his watch, but it had been confiscated along with all of his other possessions. The amount of sunlight coming in the windows told him it was at least late morning. He paced in his cell, then sat back down on the bench until he heard footsteps in the corridor.

He stood back up as Chief of Police Ross approached his cell. He looked worse than when Bolan first saw him. His eyes were red and sore from the fresh emotional wounds that had been thrust upon him. His clothes were disheveled, and the hands at his sides were gripped into tight fists. Bolan knew he was holding it together by a thread.

"Sir, I'm sorry for the loss of your son. But I need you to know that I had nothing to do with exhuming him."

There was a long pregnant pause. He leaned into the bars, his voice as coarse as if he'd tried to swallow gravel before speaking.

"Exhuming, is that what you call defiling my son's grave?"

"You must have seen my ID. I didn't fly all the way from the States to start digging up graves, sir. You can believe that or not, but I think the Undead Posse dug up your son's body to expose you and others to the same thing that killed him."

"How can that be possible?" Ross demanded. "There is no blood left in his body, and he was embalmed."

"I'm not a doctor, so I don't know. I only know what I saw, which was two of those thugs in surgical gear helping to dig up your boy. I already requested his records be examined for anything that the doctors missed, but I really think you should have the coroner take some tissue samples and send them to a lab. The guys who dug him up were wearing surgical garb and the man performing their little ceremony never touched him."

Bolan left out the part where the Obeah man was carving into his son's skin. The dark priest never made contact with the skin itself and the man didn't need that detail. It would only be another wound that could never heal.

"So you watched as all of this happened to my son?"

"I didn't like it, but yes," Bolan said. "It's part of the job sometimes."

Ross shook his head. "You should have stopped them."

"You've heard about Amber Carson, right? The senator's daughter?"

"Yes," he admitted. "She was killed in Montego Bay."

"She was drugged, raped and ritualistically murdered," Bolan countered. "But there was more to it than that. The men who did that used her to kill others back in the States. They hid an explosive device along with weaponized anthrax in her body. The weapon was detonated during her autopsy, killing several people, including Senator Carson."

"Who has ever even heard of such evil?" Ross asked. "How is it even possible?"

"This kind of men will do anything to get what they want." Bolan paused and caught the man's eyes. "I know that you don't want to believe me, but I think that you and I may have been exposed to *something,* and we need to find out what it is and fast."

An officer walked down the corridor. Ross stepped back as he spoke.

"Chief, excuse me. There is a man here from the embassy."

"Bring him here. We will see if you are telling the truth, Mr. Cooper."

The officer went back to the main desk to retrieve Anders. Bolan watched him walk down the hall with his polished leather briefcase and Armani suit. Everything about the man smelled dirty, and in most cases, Bolan wouldn't have cared, but something about Anders just made him want to snap his neck. He'd have rather tried his luck dealing with the local authorities than to rely on Anders for anything.

"Agent Cooper, I see you are already winning friends and influencing people here in Jamaica."

"So this man is truly an agent for your country?" Ross asked.

"Yes, he's one of ours."

"Then what is he doing dumping the body of my son on my doorstep?" he asked. "What kind of an agent does that?"

"Those are good questions," Anders said. "Agent Cooper?"

"I've already tried to explain. I was staking out the Undead Posse. I watched them exhume the boy while wearing surgical masks and gloves. I think they infected his body with something or were using it as a carrier. We're risking a pandemic if we don't find out what it is we're dealing with. We already know that they have a great many resources."

"Something like the Amber Carson case, you mean?" Anders asked.

"I think this may be a little more discreet, but if we've been exposed we need to find out what it is and how it is transmitted. Everyone that was in proximity to the body, or to us, could now be infected."

"You couldn't have told me this before I may have been exposed by you two?" Anders said.

"Look, I already have the boy's medical file being examined. If you can let me get to my handheld, I can tell you if they've found anything, but I recommend that the body be tested. Who knows what these guys have gotten into," Bolan said.

"I'll get the medical examiner on the phone. Christ almighty."

Bolan watched Anders stomping back down the hallway. For the most part Anders said the right things, but there was deception about him that set the soldier's teeth on edge.

Ross walked closer to the cell and leaned in and looked at Bolan, who waited as the man stared in and sized him up. He knew that Ross couldn't take much more, and he could see that he was trying to process everything that he was saying.

"What makes you think that I will believe you? I could send you so far down a hole that even the American Embassy could never get you out."

"Chief, I want the bastards as bad as you do, but if we both die from some plague because you were too stubborn to listen, then no one will get them and they will win. And, because no one here is dumb enough to take your place, and nobody else is coming down here to take my place, we're on our own."

There was another pause while Ross thought about what Bolan said, then he nodded. "Agent Cooper, I believe you. I don't know why, but I do. What do we do next?"

"I need my handheld."

The guard that was standing next to Ross went to the front to retrieve it. He looked at his boss before he handed it to Bolan in the cell. The big American powered it up and typed in his security code. He saw a message from Hal Brognola. He clicked on the note and waited for it to load. The stone walls from the jail impeded the signal.

"I need out of here so I can try to get this message."

"I can't just let you go," Ross said. "Not until we know more."

"I need to get out of this cell," he said. "The walls are interfering with the signal."

Ross reached down and unlocked the cell door. Bolan stepped out and walked down the hallway until the bars on his handheld computer indicated that the signal was strong enough.

He once again punched in the security code and the screen came to life. Bolan scrolled to the message again, pulled it up and read the information from Brognola.

"The good news is that only those who have touched the body could be infected. Direct contact is required."

"What are we potentially infected with?" Ross asked, his face a little pale in spite of his skin tone. "What have they done now?"

"That, I'm afraid, is the bad news."

Bolan's sense of humor was being tested by the gaping hospital gown he was forced to wear. Sized for a small adult, the gown left very little to the imagination and the parachuting-teddy-bear pattern was the cherry on top. The IV taped to his back and dripping antibiotics into his spinal fluid wasn't doing a lot for his mood, either.

The bacterium that they were exposed to was designed to attack the central nervous system, so the antibiotics had to go directly into the spinal fluid. Bolan knew that they had been lucky to identify the bug in time to administer the antibiotics, but he'd be happy to go the rest of his life and never get another spinal tap. There was something uniquely disturbing about having a sixteen-gauge needle jammed into one's spinal column with a popping sound that was loud enough to register in the next room. The drip finished and a nurse came in to remove the IV, which she did quickly.

"Roll over, Agent Cooper," she said. "I need you to lie flat on your back for the next forty-five minutes. That will give the medicine time to work its way into your system completely."

Bolan did as she instructed, but once she left the room,

he reached over to his bag and pulled out his cell phone. He punched in Hal Brognola's number and closed his eyes as he waited for Brognola to pick up on the other end.

"How are you feeling, Striker?" Brognola asked when he answered.

"Great," Bolan replied. "Just like a pin cushion that's been stabbed by the world's biggest needle. I've got less than an hour here, though, and I'm all set."

"The docs here say you should rest up for a few days. Stay off your feet and give your body time to heal."

"Yeah, Hal, because those killers are going to turn themselves in any minute now. I should just head down to the beach and get a mai tai."

The big Fed chuckled. "I told them that myself. They said if that was the case then to remind you that at the least you're on a no-fly for a day or so. Something about the pressure and your brain being sucked down your spinal column."

"All right, I'll keep that in mind. I don't imagine I'm flying anywhere in the next day or so anyway."

"Good. What's your next step?"

"I'm not really sure," Bolan said. "I need something concrete to go on. You got anything new for me?"

"Well, not surprisingly, the fingerprints that you sent from the cemetery all match up to known posse members. What is a surprise is that Jamaican law enforcement does a pretty good job of tracking these guys, yet do almost nothing about them. Are you sure that Jacob guy has done a Lazarus on us?"

"I'm sure," Bolan said. "It was him, large and in charge. He kept to himself mostly, but all of them seemed to be afraid of their Obeah man, which is a kind of voodoo priest. I've got a feeling that this local cop, Ross, isn't all that interested in going the law-and-order route with these guys, especially the Obeah man. He seems just as likely to cut him into small pieces and feed him to the gulls—not that I blame him. Still, it might be better overall if I can get to him first. What do you have on Ross?"

Brognola tapped keys, then said, "He looks like a pretty straight shooter, Striker. Pretty clean record, some commendations. Though I think that losing his son may be what puts him out of the police business. Some of the guys on his force down there think he's going to hang it up to protect the rest of his family."

"Understandable, but he can quit after this mission is wrapped up and these guys are put away. Until then, I need him to stick around. I'm short of allies."

"What about the local embassy guy down there, Anders?"

"He's dirty, Hal."

"You sure?" he asked, clicking away on a keyboard. No doubt he was entering data for later reference.

"There's just something not right about him," Bolan said.

"Okay, I'll put him on the watch list and see if we can pin him down on something solid. Do you need anything else?"

"Just keep feeding me intel—any kind at this point. Something about all of this isn't adding up. The thing with Ross's son makes sense, but why add a senator and his daughter into the mix? That's big business. It's one thing to try to scare off the local law dogs, but bringing U.S. law enforcement into the mix doesn't scan. Why add the pressure?"

"I agree," Brognola said. "I think you need to fill in the puzzle a bit. The story is missing some pieces. Once you find out more, get back to me, and we can compare notes… maybe put it all together."

"Will do," Bolan said, then ended the call. He heard footsteps moving down the hall and knew it was Anders even before he entered the room. He shoved the curtain aside and turned on the rest of the lights. Bolan didn't flinch at the sudden change, but noted to himself that if he had to interrogate Anders at some point to find the brightest light he could and shine it in his eyes.

"You've created one hell of a shitstorm, Agent Cooper," he said, shutting the door behind him. "I don't need messes like this."

Bolan looked straight at the man. "I'm not the one digging up corpses."

"Why didn't you stop those men?" Anders snapped. "You could have ended all of this right then and there!"

"You're wrong," he replied. "I could've captured or killed some thugs, and we wouldn't have learned anything."

"You don't seem to lack for that. They found the bodies of the other two you killed in the cemetery, and apparently there was a running gun battle when you first got into Kingston!"

Bolan looked at his watch and figured it was close enough to forty-five minutes. He sat up. "The gun battle was running all right," he said. "It was me running for my life. As far as the two in the cemetery, it was the only way to get close enough to hear what was going on. Stopping them there would have been pointless. I need to know what they are up to and how they are getting hold of such deadly biological weapons. If I'd done it then, we'd know nothing." He climbed off the table and began putting on his clothes, doing his best to ignore the slight spinning motion in his head that resulted from his movements. Buttoning his shirt, he continued. "This is a shitstorm, Anders. And it's going to get a lot worse if I don't get to the bottom of it fast."

"You're not going to be getting to the bottom of anything, Agent Cooper…or whoever the hell you really are," he said, pointing an accusing finger. "I'm revoking your right to be here. I want you on the next plane off the island."

"Then you'd best get set for some disappointment," he said. "The doc says I can't fly."

"Then you'll stay at the embassy under house arrest until

you can!" he roared at the top of his lungs. "I'm not going to have you down here making an even bigger mess of things than they already are. The posses leave the embassy alone, but with you sticking your nose into local problems you'll draw fire on us and that I cannot, and will not, allow."

Anders was huffing and puffing with the emotion of his tirade, and Bolan wasn't the least bit impressed. "You think that all of this is coincidence?" he asked. "Whose hand is in *your* pocket, Anders?"

The embassy man's face reddened in anger and his hands curled into fists. "If you weren't a spook, I'd break your fucking neck for saying that. It doesn't matter what it is, or what you think. You are done. Do you hear me, Cooper? Done." He stepped forward to shove a finger into the soldier's chest. "And don't even think about getting cute. I'll have guards posted at your door at all times. As soon as the doctor signs for you to fly, you'll be transported back to the airport and then flown back to the States. You can explain to your superiors all about the mess you've created and why U.S. international relations are in the toilet."

Anders turned on his heel and stalked out the room, slamming the door behind him. Bolan finished dressing. It was time to get out of here, since being under house arrest wouldn't serve his mission at all.

One thing was certain—this was all hitting close to home for Anders and he was getting nervous. Nervous men made mistakes, and Bolan was going to make sure that he made himself available for Anders's big debut as the villain.

THE SEDAN WAS standard embassy issue, black with tinted windows. U.S flags flickered back and forth in the wind as they drove. Bolan was technically under United States authority as long as he was in any official embassy vehicle, which worked to keep the locals at bay. The driver was armed, and appeared to have been pressed into chauffeur duty. Bolan sat in the back with Anders, though both men maintained their icy silence. Anders, presumably, because he was still angry. Bolan because he didn't have anything else to say to the man. At least not until he could prove that he was dirty. Then he'd have plenty to say.

The early-afternoon streets were busy, but Bolan knew that he'd have to make his move fast—before they were out of town—because it would be far easier to disappear into the urban sprawl of Kingston than on an empty two-lane highway. Plus, he didn't want to lose any more time in trying to get back. He allowed his gaze to pass over Anders once more. The driver appeared focused on the road.

"Want to tell me about it?" Bolan asked quietly.

Anders's head snapped around as though he'd been slapped. "Tell you about what?"

"Whatever you've gotten yourself into," he replied. "You're not the first one, you know. Happens all the time. People get sent out to do field intelligence for an embassy, it's tough, lonely work, and then they slip. Maybe they need the money or they think they're doing someone a favor and get a boot on their neck. Whatever, but it happens. This is your last chance, Anders. I'm offering you your last shot at getting out of all of this with your dignity."

"Ha, dignity! There is no dignity in politics, no dignity in serving your country. There is only the thankless job, and that's supposed to get you through the cold night. Honor and duty and all that crap. No one has a boot on my neck, Cooper," he said. "I don't know what you're talking about."

"Sure you do," he said. "I made some waves and you're already in panic mode. I can see it around your eyes and in how you twitch. Why not tell me about it?"

"There's nothing to tell, asshole," he said. "If I'm twitchy it's because of all the bullshit you've created for me to handle."

"Is that right?" Bolan asked.

"Yeah, that's right," Anders said. "So sit there and shut up."

Anders was a big man, but Bolan thought he'd been driving a desk a long time. His reflexes wouldn't be sharp. He glanced ahead and saw the intersection coming up. The timing would have to be just right.

"You believe this guy?" Bolan asked the driver, tapping him lightly on the shoulder. "He's a piece of work, isn't he?"

The driver turned his attention away from the road as the light turned red and said, "He told you to shut up." Turning his attention back, he pushed hard on the brakes to make the stop, and Bolan moved, snapping his left hand out in a sharp, chopping gesture that took Anders at the base of his throat. The big man doubled over, gagging, trying to breathe.

Bolan opened the door, then reached out and grabbed Anders by the ear, dragging him halfway across the seat as the man yowled at this new pain. Up front, the driver was struggling to put the car in Park and undo his seat belt. Stopping briefly, Bolan leaned down so Anders was certain to hear him over the car horns honking all around them at the delay.

"Listen to me, Anders. I'm going to figure this out, and I'm going to figure out your role in it. When I do, I'm coming to find you, and you'll wish you'd never heard of me. That's a promise." He gave the ear one final, hard twist, then leaped away from the car.

By then, the driver was coming around the rear, drawing his piece. "Don't do it," Bolan said, stepping forward and wrenching the man's wrist backward. He shifted his body weight, turned and face-planted him into the trunk of the car. The sound of the metal bonging on impact was almost enough to cover up the sound of the man's nose breaking. Almost.

Bolan shoved the man away, then ran across four lanes of

traffic, dodging cars and finding the nearest alley. He risked a quick look behind, but no one appeared to be following him.

Without information or allies of any kind, he was stuck. Bolan needed help, and the only person he could think of was the boy, Reggie. For the time being, he'd have to do.

There was something quite different about the Tivoli Gardens neighborhood of Kingston. As Bolan moved back through the city, avoiding the main roads and working his way through side streets and the occasional alley, he realized that it was a study in contrasts. Yes, the posses were here—gunmen and drug runners and thugs of all sorts—but there were also plenty of normal citizens just trying to get by. Which couldn't have been easy, considering that most of them lived in poverty and at the mercy of either the posses or the police—or both.

It took the better part of an hour to get back to the neighborhood he wanted, and another twenty minutes to find the hole-in-the-wall café where the boy Reggie had fed him lunch and information in exchange for lightening his wallet considerably. Bolan paused at the corner of Darling Street and Spanish Town Road, taking a quick moment to examine the large black cross monument called Lest We Forget, engraved with names that had been placed there. There were thirty-one names in all—people who had died in conflicts within the Tivoli Gardens garrison.

Bolan was as familiar with loss as anyone in the world,

and he understood that in war there would always be unexpected losses, people who died who didn't deserve to or who weren't even involved. But this neighborhood wasn't at war in any traditional sense. Even those who were in the posses were simply finding a way to build a life with the resources at their disposal. Realistically, it was no different than the young boys he'd seen joining up with militias in the Congo or those who trained at Islamic extremist terrorist camps in the remote regions of Pakistan or Afghanistan. It was inexcusable in a civilized world, but the world Bolan knew wasn't all that civilized.

He crossed the street, keeping his eyes open for police, posse members and the landmarks that would guide him back to the café. When he spotted it, he jogged across another intersection, then slipped inside the café, not even slowing until he reached a shadowed table in the back.

The curtain blocking off the kitchen twitched, and Bolan saw Reggie's grandmother peering at him from behind it, then she moved away and Reggie came out. Crossing to the table, the boy looked at him curiously.

"What brings you back here, Matt? I figured you for dead or gone."

"You bring me back, Reggie. I need your help," Bolan said. "And this time, the pay will be even better."

Suspicious, Reggie said, "What kind of help?"

Bolan looked at the boy before him and thought again about the kind of life the kid had to have had up to this point. "Reggie, what do you know about the police station?"

The kid grinned widely. "I know plenty," he said. "Been in there three or four times already."

"Good," Bolan said. "Because I'm going to need your expertise in order to get my stuff back."

WHILE MOST of Bolan's belongings had been returned to him after Chief Ross had released him, some of his more critical gear was still hidden in the car. It seemed unlikely that they'd have searched his vehicle with any care, since it was a rental. He'd have to hope he was right.

The vehicle had been impounded on a lot across the street from the police station. There was an unmanned guardhouse—likely containing the keys—inside a tall, chain-link fence and gate. The gate itself was padlocked.

From behind a garbage bin, Reggie and Bolan peered out at the arrangement once more. "It's not easy," the boy said.

"True enough," Bolan replied. "But there are no cameras that I can see, and no one on guard."

Reggie shook his head. "Someone could come out of the station at any minute. We're going to need a distraction of some kind." He leaned back against the alley wall. "It can't be you, can it?"

"No. They already know me. And it's not out of the question that they're looking for me right now."

"Then it has to be me. You will get the car," the boy said.

"Too dangerous," Bolan replied. He considered the situation carefully. "It's bad enough that I was even thinking about you getting the car. I can't be—" His words stopped as Reggie jumped to his feet and headed out of the alley at a run.

"Be ready," he called over his shoulder.

"Reggie, come back here," Bolan called, rising to go after the boy. Unfortunately, the kid was fast and was already at the mouth of the alley and hooking a left toward the station. "Damn it," he said. "Kid's going to get himself arrested."

Bolan jogged to the end of the alley, moving around the piles of trash and doing his best to ignore what he couldn't avoid. By the time he got there and peered around the corner, Bolan was just in time to see Reggie lunging up the steps of the station and beginning to scream at the top of his lungs. The soldier didn't want to see the boy get hurt, but he wouldn't waste his efforts, either.

He ran across the street and took a running leap at the fence, climbing up and over with several hard shoves from his legs. Thankful there was no barbed wire at the top, Bolan moved to the small, empty guardhouse. The door was locked, but flimsy enough, and he slammed one booted foot into it near the handle. It crashed open, revealing the interior, and a large pegboard with the key rings from each vehicle attached to it.

The keys for Bolan's rental boasted a white paper tag that read U.S. Embassy. Bolan snatched them off the pegboard and sprinted for the car, even as across the street, the sound of shouting voices could be heard, and then, ominously, a fire alarm. He pushed the button to unlock the door, then slid into the driver's seat in one smooth motion. Starting the engine, he shoved the transmission into Reverse and began backing out of the space.

Bolan looked in the rearview mirror and saw an opportunity to both help Reggie—who was standing on the steps, waving his arms wildly, and obviously looking for an escape route—and to get a little more distance between himself and Conrad Anders, who had just pulled up to a screeching halt in front of the station. Knowing that it would be only seconds before someone spotted him, Bolan shoved the gas pedal to the floor.

The eight-cylinder engine had plenty of juice and the car shot backward. He tensed as the car smashed through the gate with a metallic shriek, then braced himself as the rear bumper smashed at nearly full speed into the side of Anders's car. The sound of the impact was deafening, and in the mirror Bolan saw Anders react to the crash by throwing himself up the steps and into the crowd of milling police officers.

In the stunned silence that followed, Reggie ran down the steps and threw open the passenger door. "Go! Go!" he said.

Behind them, Bolan heard Anders shouting in rage. "Get them! Stop them! Somebody shoot that son of a bitch!"

Not waiting for the door to even close, Bolan slammed the transmission into Drive and gunned the engine again. There was a high-pitched shriek of metal as the back bumper tore free from Anders's car, then they were loose. Gunshots sounded and one shattered the back windshield as they careened down the street. "Get down, kid," Bolan snapped, shoving Reggie to the floor.

Hitting the first light at the corner, he didn't even slow, just spun the wheel and kept going. The echoes of a few last halfhearted shots sounded behind them, but he knew that for the moment, at least, they were in the clear. Reggie crawled back up into the passenger seat.

"Turn left at that set of lights," he directed. "I know a good place to hide."

Bolan nodded. "I bet you do, kid," he said. "I just bet you do."

REGGIE GUIDED Bolan out of Kingston proper and onto one of the roads leading along the beach. Resort properties and million-dollar homes competed for space, but there was no sign of the posses, and the police were far too busy in the dangerous parts of town to worry about coming out here unless they were called.

"Where are we going?" he asked.

"Turn right into the next driveway," Reggie said. "The house is empty."

"How do you know that?"

The boy shrugged. "I looked one day when I saw a for-sale sign. The house has been empty for a few months. They are trying to sell it."

"Do you come here a lot?" Bolan asked, turning into the long, curving driveway. It was lined with a dazzling white rock.

"Sometimes," the boy said. "It's nice."

Bolan pulled the car up in front of the house, then thought better of it and kept going until he saw the garage. He stopped in front of the door.

"Go see if that's open, Reggie. I want to get the car out of sight."

"Good idea, boss," he said, jumping out and running to the door. He fiddled with the handle for a minute, then held up a finger, indicating Bolan should wait. The soldier waited as the boy disappeared around the side. Sooner or later, Reggie would run into trouble, serious trouble, and that would be the end of him. The kid was smart and had good instincts, but he didn't have an ounce of caution in him.

A minute passed, then two, and just as Bolan was considering getting out to go look for the kid, the garage door rolled up on an automatic opener. "No caution," he muttered to himself. He pulled the car inside, and the door lowered behind him as he shut off the engine.

Reggie appeared at his door and then opened it with a broad gesture of welcome. "Come into the mansion, sir," he said, his already accented speech even more florid.

"Good work, Reggie," Bolan said, climbing out of the car. "Let me get some things out of the trunk, and then we'll go inside." He walked to the back of the car to inspect the damage. It was as bad as he'd feared, and the garage was empty—no tools in sight that might help open the crushed trunk. He went back to the driver's door and opened it, looking for the trunk release. It was on a small lever next to the seat on the floor.

He gave it a quick tug and heard the lock disengage. "Try to open that, Reggie," he said.

The boy pulled on the trunk, but it wouldn't budge. "Typical," Bolan said. "We're going to have to figure out something else."

Reggie grinned and opened the back door, then climbed inside. Bolan watched as he pulled down the center armrest, obviously looking for something, then pull it back. Climbing across the seat, he let out a little "ah" of pleasure, then he yanked on something, and Bolan saw the whole seat shift.

"We're lucky, boss," the boy said, climbing back out. "The seat folds down." He gave it a final shove, exposing the inside of the trunk.

"That will do it," Bolan said. "I'm not sure I'd have even thought of that."

"Don't worry about it," the boy said, a mischievous grin lighting his face. "I won't even charge you for that one!"

"I'm running up a tab?" Bolan asked, leaning into the car and working his torso into the trunk far enough for him to remove the cover over the spare-tire compartment.

"A big one," the boy replied. "Biggest one ever."

The cover came off easily enough, but underneath wasn't a spare tire, but the black case containing much of Bolan's equipment that he'd brought from the States. About the size of a large briefcase, it would come in handy as he tried to get this mission back on track. He pulled it free, dragging it after him as he exited the car.

"Let's go inside," Bolan said. "We've got work to do."

Reggie led the way from the garage and into a mudroom, which in turn led into a bright, sunny kitchen. "Welcome to my humble home," he said, laughing.

"Find a place to take a rest, kid," Bolan said. "I've got a phone call to make."

Reggie skipped across the kitchen and around the corner. Bolan pulled out his phone, looked up a number and dialed the Goldshore Villas Resort. A perky female voice answered, and Bolan asked for Robert Kowal. She asked him to hold, and a minute later, Kowal's voice picked up.

"Security, this is Robert Kowal."

"Kowal, it's Matt Cooper," he said.

"Cooper! Jesus, I wondered what happened to you. You left a dead body for me to take care of when you took off."

"Yeah, I'm sorry about that," he replied. "Truth is, I need your help. My best ally at the moment is a boy who isn't even old enough to drive yet, and I'm wanted by everyone from the Kingston police to the U.S. Embassy."

Kowal chuckled. "Well, you're either innocent or crazy, and I'm betting on innocent. Everyone on the island knows that the embassy is as corrupt as hell, and the police aren't any better. Where are you and what do you need?"

"I need backup. Can you meet me later tonight? I've got one last bit of information to put together, but then I'm going to need someone who can shoot straight and ask questions later."

The man was silent for a long minute. "All right, Cooper," he said. "I'll come. But before we go anywhere and the shooting starts, I'm going to want some better bona fides than you've given me so far."

"Done," Bolan said. "Let's meet about eleven-thirty or so."

"Just name the place," Kowal said.

Bolan gave him directions to the house he and Reggie were currently squatting in, then hung up. It was time to shorten the posse's food chain, but before he could do that, he needed more information, and there was only one man he knew for sure who could give it to him.

The vine-covered walls surrounding the grounds of Chief Ross's home hid a series of barbs and razors that Bolan hadn't anticipated. When he'd been there before, there'd been no opportunity to survey the area. While the house was outside Tivoli Gardens proper, it was still close enough to the center of Kingston for anyone to want a little added security, let alone the police chief. Patrol cars passed by regularly, and Bolan counted no less than five cruisers parked in driveways nearby. Nonetheless, the side roads approaching the neighborhood were littered with the debris from the running gun battles that the police were forced to deal with on a near constant basis from the posses. Burned-out cars filled with bullet holes and broken glass littered the alley, and would serve as barriers and hideouts the next time the two sides clashed.

Bolan had convinced Reggie to stay behind at the house and wait for Kowal, though he'd had to do some fast talking. He wanted to keep the boy out of harm's way as much as possible. He was a good kid, smart, and deserved a better life than what he'd had so far.

Above the main gate, a security camera panned back and

forth. Bolan counted silently as he determined the appropriate timing. When it reached the maximum rotation away, he broke cover and ran for the keypad, pulling out his handheld computer as he moved. Using a short USB cord attached to what looked like a plain, black rectangle of plastic like a credit card, he plugged the device into the code box. On the screen, he saw the READY message, then typed in the scan code. His handheld beeped quietly, and then the gate slid open. Bolan offered a mental thanks for the software developed at Stony Man Farm that allowed gadgets like this to work, while simultaneously wondering if the gate company might serve their clients better with more frequent and effective software updates. Far too often, electronic locks were easier to break than the old-fashioned kind.

Moving along the perimeter of the property, Bolan made his way to the back of the house, slipping from shadow to shadow. Years of experience had taught him the skill of placing his feet with silence and precision, which was why the sentry stationed near the back door didn't see or hear him. Bolan slipped a bit closer, then sprang forward, knocking the guard away from his post and into the shadow-filled yard.

The man reached for his gun, but a sharp kick knocked it away into the darkness, then Bolan was close enough to grapple. He spun the man in a tight circle, clamping down on one arm, while using his right to engage in a choke hold. The man struggled and thrashed, but was quickly unconscious.

Bolan lowered him to the ground, making sure he wasn't readily visible. Satisfied, he moved to the back door and discovered it was unlocked. He slipped inside. The back entrance led into the kitchen, and the dark expanse was dimly lit from light spilling onto the tile floor from the hallway. He paused and waited, watching the passageway. Chief Ross walked toward the kitchen, but turned away to enter a small home office. Bolan waited just long enough to ensure no entourage followed and then slipped into the room.

"What the hell!" Ross shouted.

Bolan held up his Desert Eagle as Ross reached for the phone on the small desk.

"You don't want to make that call, Chief. We need to talk." He gestured with the big gun, and Ross pulled his hand back.

"I gave you a chance, Cooper. After you used my own son against me and desecrated his body, you used violence on Anders and destroyed my impound yard." He sat down in his desk chair and pointed a long finger at him. "You're a bad man, Cooper, and I've got nothing to say to you. If you're going to use that cannon, then do it and be done with it."

"I guess that's about enough, Ross. I know you're grieving, but it's time for you to put some of that away for now. Why would I make myself sick, too? That doesn't make sense. Why would I have waited that night in front of your estate? I had time to escape and I didn't. Put on your cop hat for a minute. It doesn't add up." He took the chair across from Ross. "As for Anders, he's as dirty as old laundry water. I can't prove it yet, but I will before this is over."

Bolan watched the older man ponder his words. He could see the doubt and hesitation in the chief's eyes and knew he needed to talk fast. Jamaica was too isolated from the outside to bring in the cavalry and he really needed someone who understood the ins and outs of the island.

"Listen to me, Chief. Jacob Crisp is alive and well. He's behind all of this, and I have a feeling that Anders is running some kind of deal with him."

"You are wrong, Agent Cooper. Jacob Crisp is dead. I attended the funeral myself."

"Did you see his body?" Bolan asked. "Get a chance to check it for yourself?"

"No," he admitted, "the casket was closed."

"Take a look at this," he said, pulling his handheld computer off his belt. He used the touch screen to pull up the photos he'd taken of Crisp and the others that night in the cemetery, then passed it over to Ross.

"If you scroll through those, you'll see that Crisp is very much alive. That was how I ended up in front of your house. I was trying to follow him and get to the source."

"Why didn't you stop them from desecrating my son?" Ross held up the screen to show them lifting his son's body out of the casket. He shook as he stood and rested one hand on the desk supporting his weight and the other arm extended with the gruesome pictures. Bolan knew that he had to trust someone, and Ross was his best hope.

"We've been over this—I couldn't stop them because of what happened with Amber Carson."

"Yes, I know…" Ross said.

"When I saw them digging up your son's body, I believed that they were going to try to do something similar with you, and I was right, but this time it wasn't anthrax, it was something a little more subtle. They're testing right now, but when they're done testing, I can't imagine what they'll do." Bolan shrugged and settled the Desert Eagle back in its holster. "With you out of the way, Anders and Crisp know that there will be little interference from the local police, because no one else wants to take them on."

"And that was why you stayed. You were trying to prevent them from killing me with my own son. Even now, they have managed to have us fighting each other." Ross stood up and Bolan watched him carefully. His eyes were brighter, and he radiated a stronger energy. "I've long suspected Anders was dirty myself, but I could never prove it. Even if I could, it is unlikely that anyone in the United States would listen to me."

"I'm still trying to figure out how Anders is orchestrating

all of this," Bolan admitted, "but it's got to be him. Crisp doesn't have those kinds of resources on his own. No way."

"No, I'm afraid you are wrong, Agent Cooper. Anders holds no real power here on the island. With Crisp still alive, it is certain that he is running Tivoli Gardens and maybe other garrisons, as well. There has never been a more powerful posse leader. Let me show you this."

Ross pulled a file from his drawer and opened it on the desk. He fanned the pictures that were in the file out in front of Bolan. The theme for the pictures was a wooden doorway with ropes dangling down and tied in loops at the end. Three men hung in the loops from their arms, strips of skin hung from their backs and legs and the ground was a giant pool of blood.

"This is the penalty for anyone who is believed to have conspired against Jacob Crisp.

"This man here—" he pointed to the third corpse in the picture "—was his cousin. We arrested him and he led us to a minor stash of drugs, barely enough to bring a charge, but enough for Crisp to do away with him."

Bolan scanned the pictures. Some of the victims had been whipped, others bludgeoned with a bat. One photo was of a corpse that had been set aflame. Bolan read the information next to it: Unknown fifteen-year-old. Cause of Death: Burned.

"You see, Agent Cooper, Jacob Crisp is not a fearful man, or a cautious one. Somehow, he is running things—at least here in Jamaica."

"What about this Obeah man?" Bolan asked.

"He lives outside the city, in a hut in the jungle. Most people fear him." Ross chuckled softly. "Obeah is a good reason for most people to be afraid. His followers are loyal, and true believers will do anything to gain the kind of power that he promises."

"You don't sound convinced."

"Once you have seen these kinds of things," he said, pointing to the pictures, "the idea of dark magic cannot be any worse than the evil that already exists. Obeah, Crisp and Anders are all cut from the same cloth. They use fear and power to gain what they want and have no conscience to act as an adviser to their soul."

"I can't disagree with you there, Chief. I'm going to pay Crisp's Obeah man a visit. With a little application of my own form of magic, maybe he'll tell me what we need to know."

"I can give you directions, but I urge you to be cautious. It is almost as easy to dismiss the things you do not understand than to fear the things you do. I do not fear the Obeah man because I have nothing left in this world to lose. But he is dangerous—of that I'm sure—and his apprentice, the man they call Spook, even more so." Ross leaned forward and offered his hand, which Bolan took and shook gladly. "If there is anything else I can do, I will."

"For now, it'd be nice if you'd tell your men to stop looking for me," Bolan said. "I've got enough problems to deal with."

Ross laughed again. "Indeed you do, Agent Cooper. Indeed you do. I will see to it that the Kingston police do not interfere with you. I cannot, however, act to stop anyone from the embassy."

"If anyone from the embassy comes, I'll deal with them myself."

AFTER GETTING DETAILED directions from Chief Ross, and helping the sentry get to an ice pack, Bolan returned to the mansion by the sea to find Rob Kowal sitting on the tailgate of a truck in the driveway. He held a cola in one hand and was chatting with Reggie, who also held a cola. They appeared to be getting along famously.

He pulled the car to a stop and got out. “Kowal,” he said. “Thanks for coming.”

“Call me Rob,” the man said, getting to his feet and offering his hand. “I had a feeling you’d found trouble.”

Bolan shook hands, then nodded. “Trouble with a capital *T*,” he said. “The Undead Posse is working out ways to deliver even more bioweapons into the United States, and they’re getting creative with their choices. The last one they tested would have killed me if I hadn’t figured it out in time.”

“That’s trouble, all right,” he said, “but why not use the embassy or your own CIA resources for help? I’m not active anymore.”

“Anders is dirty,” Bolan said. “He’s involved in it all somehow. I just haven’t tied him down yet. And getting help here from the States would take too long. I want to move tonight, see if I can press them.” He stared hard at the ex–Secret Service agent. “So I called you. If you don’t want to be in the middle of a mess, then you should probably leave now, but I could use the extra set of eyes and the extra firepower.”

“Fair enough. Suits, ties and sitting behind a desk aren’t exactly my specialty,” he said. “Where are we going?”

Bolan explained about the Obeah man and the location of his house. “I figure we go out there and have a friendly talk with him.”

“Oh, you want to be friendly,” Kowal said, laughing. “Why didn’t you say so?”

“I’m always friendly,” Bolan said. “I’m the patron saint of friendly.”

“Yeah, I saw the result of your friendly talks on the body you left in my parking lot,” Kowal said. “But I’m guessing these guys don’t play nice.”

“Not a bit,” Bolan said.

"What are you going to do with the boy?" he asked, gesturing at Reggie who'd watched the exchange carefully.

"He's going to stay here," Bolan said firmly.

"But I'm—" Reggie began, but was cut short when Bolan gave him a sharp look.

"You're going to stay here because I say so," Bolan said sternly. He picked him up and carried him into the house. Kowal followed along behind and watched as Bolan set Reggie on the carpeted living-room floor.

"Okay, okay. I'll stay put," Reggie said.

"He's a good kid and I don't want to see him killed," Bolan said, as he and Kowal left the house.

Kowal was silent for a moment, then nodded. "Yeah, I get that. Nice to see one that wants to do the right stuff. We don't have enough like that anymore, especially in places like this. Hope he keeps to this path and doesn't get himself killed."

"Agreed," Bolan said, thinking of the atrocities committed by Jacob Crisp and his posse members. "Let's see what we can do about that. At least for this neighborhood." He turned and headed back outside, glad that for this night at least, Reggie would be safe.

And the Executioner could do the work that needed to be done.

Bolan moved his gear to the scaled-down Hummer that Kowal was driving. While the sedan was inconspicuous, it wasn't out of the question that the road would be rough. Once underway, it took the better part of an hour to cross Kingston and get back out of the city, working along the coast toward the southeast and an area marked on the map as Bull Bay.

Most of the buildings along the A4 highway were run-down slums, many of which had been washed over by mud slides at some point in the past. Still, there were signs that people were trying to live in these places. It never failed to amaze Bolan, for all his travels, that in a world with so much wealth, people were still living in slums and eating out of trash cans. The moon was half-full and shone on the water, which was still and calm.

There was plenty of beauty in Jamaica—resorts practically built of gold, lavish estates, extravagant food and liquor. And then just around the corner, out of sight, were places like this or slums like the one Reggie haunted. It didn't make sense that there could be such disparity in one place, that those who had so much would do so little for those who had almost nothing, but it was true the world over.

Kowal drove confidently and—much to Bolan's pleasant surprise—he kept quiet. He wondered about the man who had agreed to risk his neck.

"What made you leave the Secret Service?" Bolan asked.

"I had the realization that I was tired of being a target without a voice. Depending on the commander at the time, how we approached different assignments changed. My last supervisor made it clear that there was no room for independent thinking. I'd been a field agent for too long and that didn't work. Organizations can't function properly if you don't let people do what they need to do. But you know how that story goes, being CIA and all, right?"

"Well, CIA is my cover this time. I assume you've made some phone calls."

"I've made some calls," he admitted. "But while lots of people know of you, no one I know *knows* you. Everyone says you're on the home team, some kind of specialist. But no one appears to know which agency you actually play for."

"I play for the United States of America," Bolan said seriously. "My job is to do the job, no matter what it takes. I can't connect directly with an official agency, because all of the red tape is not conducive to getting things done. If you're always busy following the rules, but the bad guys aren't, it's easy for them to stay one step ahead."

"So then CIA is a cover? A ghost pretending to be a spook… Interesting."

"Something like that," he said.

Kowal turned and focused on the road, and that allowed Bolan the time to consider the best approach to getting the Obeah man to talk. From time to time, he glanced up at the road and then at the scribbled directions he'd received from Chief Ross. When he saw the turnoff, he said, "Turn left here."

Kowal did as instructed, and Bolan guided him to a burned-out building about a quarter of a mile off the main highway. "We'll walk from here," he said. "There's no point in announcing our presence too soon."

"Agreed," Kowal said, shutting down the engine. "What's the plan?"

"The place we're looking for is just under half a mile from here, according to what Ross told me," he said. "Once we're closer, we'll choose a plan of attack." He climbed out of the Hummer and moved to the back. "Let's gear up."

Kowal joined him, and Bolan opened his field case. He gave the other man a secure com unit for his ear and put another one in his own. "Check?" he asked quietly into the microphone piece.

"Check," Kowal replied.

Bolan then removed two fresh magazines for his Desert Eagle. "What kind of weapon are you carrying?" he asked.

Kowal opened his coat to reveal his shoulder holster. "SIG-Sauer P-229, with .357 rounds."

"That'll do," Bolan said. "I'm hoping to do this quietly, without any gunplay, but if it comes to it, remember that these people are killers. They won't hesitate to take you out."

"I know," the other man said. "Let's just get it done."

Bolan nodded and finished gearing up, then turned and led the way, heading off the road and into the dense overgrowth beside it.

THE OBEAH MAN lived in a whitewashed stone house that had once been servants' quarters of some kind. It lay hidden behind overgrown trees and debris, in the shadow of a nearby larger structure that was a colonial remnant and looked more like an old fort that had been under attack than a house. Graffiti was spray-painted on the walls, and the windows were broken out and boarded over in some places. Giving the building a quick once-over, Bolan decided that with the crumbling walls around the property and the general state of disrepair, it looked like a haunted house. No doubt the effect was intentional.

There was a driveway, lined with exotic plants and stacks of animal bones topped with bleached-out skulls. The wind shifted slightly, and there was a sudden smell in the air of blood and something rotting. This was a place that had seen a lot of death and terror. Bolan had smelled and felt the same exact thing in places in Africa and the Middle East. He motioned for Kowal to stop, and they knelt in the tall grass.

"Here," Bolan said, handing over a small shoulder bag. "I know you've got the SIG, but just in case, I took the liberty of bringing you some backup hardware."

Kowal looked inside the bag and grinned. "Aww… And I didn't get you anything."

"Remember, I want to keep this quiet and nonlethal if possible," he said. "Fast and efficient."

"Got it. Which side do you want me on?"

"You'll take the front entrance, and I'll go through the back. According to Ross, there's not much to this place, so they'll have to come one way or the other. For now, let's get a little closer and see what we've got."

"Good enough for me," the other man said. "I don't suppose you know what that smell is?"

"Blood and guts," Bolan said shortly. "It smells the same here as it does everywhere else—bad. God knows what they're up to in there, so stay sharp."

"Always do," Kowal said.

They snuck through the trees and approached the house. The drive was filled with various cars, many of them spray-painted in posse symbols, including a massive black hearse. Bolan signaled for Kowal to follow him as they sidled up to the car parked at the farthest end of the drive. Four sentries were posted along the driveway itself, all of them armed.

They didn't seem to be patrolling, just standing guard, and from the look of it, not paying that much attention.

"Two by two," Bolan whispered, and Kowal nodded in agreement.

Moving silently, they crept in behind the two closest sentries. Bolan signaled that Kowal should take the one on the far left, and the man slipped away, as the soldier closed in on his own target. Removing a combat knife from his boot, Bolan struck swiftly, wrapping his arm around the man from behind and covering his mouth to stifle his shout of warning, even as he slammed the blade home near the man's spine, paralyzing him instantly. Out of the corner of his eye, he saw Kowal finish off his own target.

They had to have made at least some noise, because the second set of guards began moving down the driveway. One of them called out a name—probably one of the dead men—but before he could sound the alarm, Bolan pulled a thin throwing blade from his belt and sent it spinning across the distance into the man's throat. He pitched over backward with a soft gurgle.

The second was a little farther away, but Kowal moved fast. The surprise was still on the sentry's face as the ex–Secret Service agent closed in and snapped his neck in one quick jerk.

They moved their victims out of sight and began to circle the house. A small window at the back of the building revealed the Obeah man with his latest victim.

Four men stood around a large, heavy table. In the center of the table, a girl was stripped of her clothing and tied down. The Obeah man began to chant, then took out a scalpel and sliced a thin line down her arm. The girl cried out in pain, and Bolan felt Kowal stiffen beside him. The cry was a shock—he'd assumed she was drugged—but it was too much for the man beside him, who was already in motion.

Somehow, Bolan managed to snag his arm at the last second before he went bursting through the door.

He leaned in close enough so that Kowal would hear his almost inaudible words. "White knights usually get themselves killed. Stick to the plan and go to the front."

"But she—"

"Will die first if we do this wrong. Now move out and wait for my signal."

Bolan felt the other man tense, then relax. Kowal nodded and moved toward the front of the building. After waiting several long minutes for him to get into place, Bolan positioned himself at the door, then spoke softly into his mike.

"Set?"

"Set," the reply came.

"Three…two…one…go!"

Bolan burst through the back door as Kowal went through the front. The house was barely more than a two-room shack, and they could see each other clearly enough across the space. Between them was the main open room where the girl was being tortured.

One of the men had climbed onto the table with his pants lowered. Bolan and Kowal both fired simultaneously. The force of the bullets sent the perpetrator flying through the air like an out-of-control marionette.

"Kill them!" the Obeah man screamed as he fell to the floor, crawling away. Two men entered from another room to the side, and the space filled with the smell of gunpowder as everyone used the walls for cover.

Knowing the walls were stone, Bolan opted for planned shots. He waited until the two of the men in the main room exposed the toes of their shoes, then fired two quick shots in succession. Both men screamed and stood up, and Kowal mowed them down before they had the chance to seek cover again.

The girl on the table was screaming in a high-pitched

wail, and the third man stood up to provide cover for the Obeah man, who ran for the next room, even as his bodyguard died to protect him. The two men in the other room covered his retreat and were apparently holed up and ready to make a stand long enough for reinforcements to arrive.

"Damn it," Bolan said. "They're in there as tight as sardines."

Just then, a small explosion rocked the house to its foundation. The sound of rock hitting the ground outside told Bolan everything he needed to know. They'd blown a hole in the outside wall to make their escape.

He and Kowal entered the main room, as the men holding the doorway began to retreat. The last posse member in the doorway took a hit to the thigh, but slipped out of sight into the dark room before Bolan could finish him off

Kowal pulled out a knife and began to cut the girl free. "I'll get her to safety," he said. "You go find those bastards and kill them."

Bolan nodded and bounded through the doorway. He took two steps before a bullet clipped his left shoulder, knocking him off balance. Rather than force the movement, he followed the kinetic energy down and rolled sideways. The second bullet made a buzzing sound as it went over his head and lodged into the door frame.

He stayed tucked down and grabbed a pressure dressing out of his pocket, shoving it up underneath his shirt. By feel, he quickly assessed the wound and determined that it wasn't serious. A good scratch that another inch or two in would have been a major problem. He left the dressing in place to staunch the bleeding, then wiped his blood-slicked hands on his BDU pants. Popping a new magazine into the Desert Eagle, he waited, knowing that there were still more posse members out there, but not precise locations.

And the Obeah man had vanished.

A crash in the front room gave Bolan a place to start. He

moved along the wall and saw that Kowal and the girl were gone, but now a posse member was making his way into the back door. Bolan didn't quite have the angle, but he sent two shots into the man's leg. The posse member screeched and reached over to grab his injured limb.

Bolan took the shot and sent a round through his head, silencing him immediately. Outside, he heard an engine rev and knew he was about to lose his target. A moving shadow was all the warning he had, and he did a full, running roll to get out of the way as a machete glinted in the moonlight.

"Got to kill you, blood clot," the heavily accented voice said. "For the Obeah man."

Bolan kept moving and came up with the Desert Eagle in his hand. He needed someone left alive who could talk, so he fired low, blowing out the man's kneecap.

He screamed and went down, and Bolan turned back to the driveway, hoping to catch up. The car tires kicked up gravel as the vehicle peeled away, and he got only a glimpse inside. The man they called Spook was at the wheel, and the Obeah man was in the passenger seat next to him.

Bolan turned back to the man screaming on the ground and kicked the machete out of reach. "We need to have a talk," he said, gripping the thug by the ankle and dragging him back inside the shot-up house.

Between the gunshot wound and being dragged back inside by a wrenched knee, the posse member had passed out. While waiting for Kowal to return, Bolan had tied the man to a chair using a combination of a lamp cord and a torn-up sheet from the ratty bedroom. His hands were secured behind his back, and his ankles were placed on the outside of the legs of the chair and tied sideways, thus minimizing any leverage he might have once he woke up.

Bolan surveyed the room and walked up to the split wooden frame with the bullet embedded deep within it. He rubbed his shoulder and contemplated how many bullets had been intended for him over the years.

He moved some debris out of the way. Several minutes after he finished, Kowal returned.

"The one that didn't get away?" he asked, giving a nod in the unconscious man's direction.

Bolan looked at the immobile posse member. His black hair was done in long dreadlocks that hung almost to the middle of his back, and there were little talismans of some kind woven into the strands. He wore tattered jeans and a black T-shirt with a red Aerosmith emblem on it. Both of his ears were pierced, as was his nose, and there was a series of rings twisted through his eyebrows. At a guess, the man hadn't shaved in a few days, and he smelled as if his last shower had been several days or even weeks before that. He wore Converse high tops that were lime green.

"A real fashion statement," Bolan said. "He's what… twenty-five at most?"

"I'd guess younger," Kowal said. "What a waste."

Bolan thought about Reggie. If something didn't change for him soon, it was possible, maybe even likely, that he'd wind up in a posse himself. "I imagine he thought it was his only choice. Work with the posses or die by them."

"Probably," the man admitted, drawing a large pan full of rusty tap water in the sink. "But plenty have come from worse and done better with themselves."

"True enough," Bolan admitted. "Let's wake him up."

Kowal brought the pan of water and threw it into the face of the Undead Posse member. He sputtered and stirred. "Did you treat his bullet wound?" he asked.

"Not yet," he replied. Bolan reached into his pack and pulled out a pressure bandage and tossed it to Kowal. The bullet had passed through the outer fat and muscle of the thug's thigh. He pressed the bandage into place, then took one of the remaining strips of sheet lying nearby and wrapped it around the wound, tying a tight knot directly over the hole.

"Ahhh. What the hell?"

"Oh, look! Our friend is awake," he said.

Bolan leaned back against the table in front of his prisoner. He watched as the blood oozed through the bandage and began to drip onto the floor. He looked back up at the posse member, a question on his face.

"What you think? You think that a little bleeding gonna scare me? You don't know who the fuck you're dealing with." He struggled against his bonds for a moment. "But you will, white man."

"Here's what I know," Bolan began. "I know that you guys were using this place as a body chop shop. It smells like an abattoir. I also know that you're going to tell me everything that you know about the Obeah man, Spook and Jacob Crisp."

"That what you think, man."

Bolan leaped forward and slammed a heavy fist into the leg wound, twisting on it as hard as he could. The posse member screamed in pain and Bolan leaned back once more.

"Let's start with something easy," he said. "What's your name?"

"Bob Marley, who the fuck you think!"

"I don't know," Bolan said, resuming his position against the table. "The way that thing is bleeding, I think maybe I nicked an artery or something. You could bleed to death over all this."

"Anton…" he said sullenly. "My name is Anton."

"See, Anton, that wasn't so difficult," he said.

"Isn't cooperation fun?" Bolan asked Kowal.

The man nodded. "More fun than bleeding to death, for sure."

Bolan looked at Anton once more. "Anton, you're going to tell me what's going on with the Undead Posse. And you're going to tell me now."

"I *can't* tell you, man. No matter what you do to me. The Obeah man will curse me and me parts will fall off. Or the Spook will get me. Take me to jail, man, but I can't disobey 'dem."

Bolan shook his head. This time, he leaned forward and tore the pressure bandage away, then jammed a thumb into the bleeding holes just enough to make Anton feel the pain. Bolan would never go too far, but there was no need to let Anton in on that bit of information.

"You need to understand, Anton. I'm not that kind of law. I don't take people to jail, but I don't have a problem getting them to the cemetery. The Obeah man or Spook *might* kill you...but I *will*. So talk—fast—or you'll be praying that your posse comes back to kill you." He leaned back, catching the rag Kowal tossed him and wiping off his hands. In the chair, Anton was sweating like a hard-run horse and panting with exertion. "Now talk, Anton, before I have to resort to really painful methods of getting your attention."

The man's shoulders sagged in defeat. "I only know the last girls we brought here. The one you took away was supposed to be special, like that Amber girl the Spook killed. That's why she wasn't dead yet. The Obeah man, he said we must bless her with our seed and that is what makes the magic work. Then they sacrifice her and add in the special stuff. The others will be sent when the time is right."

"Others?" Bolan asked sharply.

"They got some downstairs already filled with the special stuff. We're not supposed to disturb them. Too dangerous."

"Show me," Bolan demanded.

Kowal reached down and cut the man's restraints. Anton rubbed his wrists and glared at his two captors. "Don't even think it," Kowal growled as he grabbed the back of the chair and lifted it, knocking Anton forward into Bolan, who grabbed him by the shoulders and spun him.

"Move," he said, shoving him toward the other room.

Anton limped through the short hallway and into the bedroom. Inside, he lifted a rug, revealing a trapdoor.

"There," he said, "now let me go. If I leave soon, then the Obeah man may not strip my soul and feed it to the demons."

"I don't think so. Open it."

Bolan and Kowal stepped back and when Anton hesitated, Bolan drew his Desert Eagle. "If it's a trap, I think I'd rather have you with a lungful of anthrax than us."

“I need your knife,” Anton said to Kowal.

“I need a new Ferrari,” he replied, “but I’m not fucking getting one, and you’re not getting this.” He held up the knife to illustrate his point.

“There’s a cord, man,” he said. “If I don’t cut it, we all die.”

“Here,” Bolan said, handing him a small throwing blade. “Don’t get any funny ideas.”

“Yeah, man, you the badass,” Anton said. He knelt on the floor, then slid it between the boards, releasing the hidden spring. He set the knife aside and stood to open the door. The opening led to a root cellar. Not a popular item on islands that flooded, but considering the date of the house not uncommon. Bolan nudged him down the stairs. The only part of the cellar that still looked original were the beams on the ceiling. The floor was poured concrete, fluorescent lights lit the room, and three metal cadaver gurneys lined the walls, each hosting a body. Bolan pulled back the sheets to see the young women that had been violated. Each face told a different story. One was definitely local, one he thought he recognized as another politician’s daughter and the last looked like the typical girl next door.

He heard Anton moving behind him. Bolan ducked as the board swung past his head. He landed a solid punch to Anton’s solar plexus. The man scrambled backward and stretched to reach a vial on the mayo stand. Bolan leaped forward, grabbed his arm and spun him. The posse member continued to struggle, slamming the back of his head into Bolan’s cheek and nearly crushing his nose.

Shoving a knee into Anton’s back, Bolan wrapped an arm around the man’s chin, while his other hand grasped the back of his head. A sharp twist and Anton’s neck snapped. The sound was like stepping on a branch in the wintertime.

From behind him, Kowal asked, “Do you kill everyone you meet?”

"No, but I admit that it can seem that way sometimes." He gestured to the steps. "Let's get topside. These guys don't appear to be the most conscientious about hazmat protocols."

They climbed the stairs and Bolan punched Brognola's contact number.

"Striker, you got good news for me?" the big Fed asked.

"Well, since I have another dead daughter of a politician and several other corpses, I would say no, not good news."

"You know, I'm going to stop taking your phone calls if they're all going to sound like this. Who's the girl?"

"Don't know her name, but I recognize her. You'll have to send a hazmat team to go through all of this. There are traps, and one of the posse members said that the girls are already filled with contaminants," Bolan explained. "I'm sending you the coordinates, just get the teams here and send some bomb people with them, as well. And, Hal, get the State Department to put up some travel restrictions for this part of the world. I really don't need extra bodies complicating things more."

"They'll be there soon."

"Thanks, Hal."

Bolan walked back over to Kowal. "Maybe you should let your friends in the Secret Service in on this stuff," Bolan said after a moment's thought. "This could get ugly fast."

"What makes you say that?" Kowal asked.

"Because I've seen one of those kids down there before—she's related to a politician, I just can't remember the name. Someone is trying to make an example out of our government, and they should have their heads up. My contact will let people know through more official channels, but that could take way too long. We don't know when or where they've sent bodies."

"Agreed," he said. "Let me go make a call."

Kowal walked outside with his cell phone. Bolan started

searching the rest of the house, looking for more information. He heard a footstep behind him and spun, drawing the Desert Eagle.

Reggie's eyes went wide at the sight of the big gun and held up his hands. "Hey, don't shoot me, boss man. I'm on your side."

Bolan holstered his pistol. "Reggie, what are you doing here? This place is dangerous."

"I came to help. What ya lookin' for?"

"I'm looking for a direction," he said. "Any direction."

"What you mean?"

"I mean, I have to find this Obeah man and that Spook character. They got away. You have any ideas?" He scanned the room once more and saw nothing of interest.

Reggie thought about it. "Yeah, I can help you. These guys, they aren't normal posse, are they?"

Bolan chuckled. "Normal posse? What does that even mean, kid?"

"There's a lot of posses in Kingston. They run drugs or weapons, but they also help out the garrison. You know, food and medicine and stuff."

"No, then these guys aren't normal. Not unless you think spreading dangerous diseases is normal."

Reggie should his head. "No way. There's rules and all. That's how they all survive. If the posse only fights the government and they help us out on occasion, everyone just leaves them alone, but when they start hurting all the people then there is no place for them to hide."

"I don't think these guys are following any rules but their own," Bolan said. "So, how can you help?"

"This one's free," the boy said. "The Spook has a house in Montego Bay. Out by the water. I took a delivery there once. I can show you where it is."

Bolan shook his head, wondering what the kid would have been delivering clear over in Montego Bay, then decided it would be better not to ask. "You can show me," he said, "on a *map*."

Kowal stepped back inside. "I've let the proper people know."

"Good. They'll be ready?" Bolan asked.

"Always, but they appreciated the heads-up," he replied, looking with interest at the sudden appearance of the boy. "What's he doing here, and what's our next move?"

"Montego Bay," Bolan and Reggie answered at the same time.

Before Kowal could make a comment, Bolan said, "Let's move," and walked out the door, leaving the slaughterhouse behind.

13

The drive back to Montego Bay wasn't particularly long, but it gave Bolan plenty of time to think. While Jamaica was known as one of the most beautiful vacation destinations in the world, he had more on his mind than bikinis and beach balls. Not the least of which was the boy sitting in the back, jabbering about this and that with Kowal. He glanced at Reggie in the rearview mirror. He had planned on leaving him in Kingston, but the kid seemed to have almost unlimited local resources and knowledge. Bolan had intercepted him while he was trying to set up a ride that would take him to Montego Bay. Giving up, Bolan finally told him that he may as well come along, so at least he could keep an eye on him. And, he'd have a better shot of keeping Reggie alive if he knew where he was.

They turned onto the road that would take them to the estate, and Bolan slammed on the brakes. Undead Posse marked cars were parked all along the street, right up to the gate. They'd be as thick as thieves and armed to the teeth. He quickly backed up and started to park. He'd have to find a way to sneak around the armed militia that was guarding Spook and the Obeah man.

"Hey," Reggie said, tapping him on the shoulder. "What are you doing?"

"I've got to find somewhere to hide the car, then Kowal and I will try to make our way inside without getting shot. You'll stay here and wait." Bolan turned to give the boy a hard stare. "And this time I mean it."

"You mainlanders," Reggie said with a laugh. "You know nothing about island ways. Go back to the last resort we passed."

"What for?" Bolan asked.

"Trust me," Reggie said, grinning.

"If I had a dime for every time I've heard that," Bolan said, shaking his head. But since he didn't have a clever solution, and the boy had more than proved his worth, he turned the car and went to the beach resort that was a mile back down the road. They parked and Reggie jumped out of the car, slamming the door behind him.

The kid was halfway to the main building when he turned back. "What are you two sitting there for? Come on."

Bolan and Kowal got out of the car and followed Reggie into the hotel.

"You have any idea what he's up to?" Kowal asked quietly.

"Not a clue," Bolan admitted. "But let's see what he comes up with."

The hotel wasn't a resort condo like the one Amber Carson had been staying at, but more of a typical hotel by the sea. It was an older building that had seen better days. The exterior had been upgraded, but the interior looked like an old Las Vegas casino with wall-to-wall red carpet that was worn black in some places, and smoky glass lined the walls at the entrance.

Reggie walked up to the main desk. "Hey, man, I got two tourists with lots of money and no idea what they're doing.

I told them I could land us a couple of Jet Skis for a night cruise in the bay."

The clerk shook his head. "Now, boy, you know we only be dealing with guests."

Bolan walked up to the desk and pulled out his CIA credentials, satisfied when the man's eyes got a little white around the edges. Then he reached into his coat and pulled out five one-hundred-dollar bills. "Think of me as a guest," he said, "and that will be three Jet Skis if you've got them."

THE WATER WAS blessedly warm and calm. Rather than travel directly down the coastline, Bolan steered the small craft in a fairly large arc, allowing them to approach the small dock on the shore behind Spook's house from the ocean. A hundred yards out, he cut the engine and the others did the same.

"We'll push them in from here," he said. "Move with the waves—shorter movements will be harder to see."

"I'm just thankful there are no shore lights," Kowal said. "I just had those installed at the Goldshore."

"They don't want people to see them," Bolan said, "which works in our favor."

They began working toward the dock, letting the waves carry them forward, until they reached the dock, then slipped beneath. "We'll tie them up here," he said, using a nylon rope attached to the small craft to secure it to one of the support posts. The other two followed suit.

"Okay," he whispered. "There's plenty of cover up along the shore. Move quietly." They tucked into the sea oats on top of a dune. The tall plants that resembled wheat were thick enough to hide their shapes, but not so thick that they obscured their view. Bolan pulled out his spotting scope and perused the beach and then the house.

"Damn," Bolan said, pitching his voice low.

"What is it?" Kowal asked.

"It's a full house," he said. "Crisp, Spook and the Obeah man are all there, along with some of their thugs. But who I don't see is Anders. I was sort of hoping to get all of the fish in one big barrel."

"Since when is anything in this business convenient?"

"True enough," Bolan admitted, then he turned to Reggie. "Since I know you won't stay out of this, I have a job for you, though you may not like it very much."

"Name it, boss," the boy said.

Bolan couldn't help but grin at him. The boy had more game than a lot of grown men he'd dealt with over the years. "They've got a full-blown fortress here," he said, "and if I'm going to get to the ones who count, we're going to have to separate them from the other posse members."

"Makes sense," Reggie said. "We do that all the time in the market when we want to steal fruit."

"Glad you understand," Bolan said. "So what we're going to do is get their attention, and when I signal you, I want you to make a run for the Jet Skis and take off. Make lots of waves and noise and head out into the ocean a ways."

"They'll come after me," he said, looking doubtful.

"I hope so," he said. "That will give me a chance to take some of the posse members out from the beach."

Reggie nodded. "Just don't let them kill me," he said in all earnestness. "My grandma is counting on me to pay the rent and stuff."

"You'll be safe," Bolan said.

He turned to Kowal. "I want you to take a position on that set of dunes at three o'clock. When we've cleared the road, I'll go in, but I want you to stay put in case they've got others who are coming in behind me."

"What about out in front on the road?" Kowal asked. "There's bound to be some out there."

"I'll take care of that," Bolan said. He opened his equipment case and began putting together the Tavor assault rifle.

Putting aside the regular magazine, he selected one loaded with tracer rounds.

"What are those funny red-tipped ones?" Reggie asked, peering at them curiously.

"Tracers," Bolan said shortly. "They'll act as markers for our position, as well as help me spot the posse members."

"Why do you want to tell them where you are?" the boy asked, his voice a little panicky.

"It's like trying to lead a mouse through a maze," he said. "First, you've got to show them the cheese." Bolan checked the rifle one last time, then his Desert Eagle, and nodded to himself. "Now get to the bottom of the dune. I'm going to fire three rounds. When the first spotlights head our way, I want you to take off. I'll make sure they don't get near you."

"Okay."

Reggie moved to the bottom of the dune at the same time as Kowal took up his position. Once they were in place, Bolan keyed his mike.

"Ready for some action, Rob?"

"Just like riding a bike," he replied. "In hell."

Bolan took up a prone position, using the tripod to steady the barrel of his weapon. The rifle poked out a short distance through the waving yellow plants he was using for cover. Snugging the rifle into his shoulder, he peered through the scope and scanned the house for first-shot possibilities.

He could see three guards patrolling the rear of the house, and it was likely that there would be an equal or greater number in the front. Moving his view to the large windows designed to offer a breathtaking ocean view—but instead offered Bolan an all-access view of the great room and part of the kitchen—he could see all three of the men he truly wanted to take out.

"Stand by, Rob," he said.

"Affirmative," the reply came.

Bolan switched his radio frequency to the local police

band, something he'd noticed earlier in the jail. Keying the mike he said, "Shots fired in the North Shore area. Repeat—shots fired. Send backup."

Knowing this would bring every police officer in the area on the run, he switched back to the frequency he was using with Kowal, then took aim.

On the other side of the glass, Crisp was lifting a drink to his lips. Bolan exhaled smoothly and waited for cross-hairs to steady, then squeezed the trigger. There was a barely perceptible widening of Crisp's eyes as the tracer shattered the window, Crisp's glass and hurtled into the bodyguard standing in front of him. The impact of the bullet knocked the man off his feet as tiny flames flickered on his jacket. Crisp hit the dirt, as did Spook and the Obeah man, which was exactly where Bolan wanted all three of them—scared and looking for cover until he could get there.

Bolan recentered and delivered the next round into another posse member who was in the living room, leaning against the fireplace. Then he turned his attention from the great room to the front of the house and picked off one of the guards as they ran to get in on the action.

A spotlight flared to life at the house and began to scan the dunes. Bolan looked over his shoulder and shouted, "Run, Reggie!"

The boy didn't need any greater encouragement. He kicked up the sand as he ran. One patrol from farther down the beach began to open fire. Bolan focused the scope and took out one and then the other in quick succession. Reggie didn't stop running.

Bolan heard Kowal beginning to shoot just before automatic gunfire began to spray from the guards patrolling the back of the house. Bolan tucked down on the dune and shook his head. Typical fools with guns and not a lot of combat sense. These weren't soldiers, but inner-city thugs with nothing better to do than fight and join a posse. That didn't change their willingness to kill, just their ability in a basic combat scenario. Bolan slid forward again and popped off the last two tracer rounds, one into the lead gang member who was headed his way and the last he saved for the spotlight. He popped the magazine and rammed home a new one.

He heard Kowal laying down cover fire. Bolan slid to the bottom of the dune and made it to Kowal's position before the posse members were able to get another light scanning the beach.

"I forgot how exciting this can be," Kowal said. "Haven't had this much fun since I left the Rangers and went into the Secret Service."

"Never a dull moment," Bolan replied. "Ready?"

"Always," he said. "Let's mow the lawn."

Bolan and Kowal opened up on the posse members who were heading their way. They began to turn and run, but lights and sirens were moving toward the house. The posse began to scatter, looking for places to hide or ways to escape. The rats were stuck in the maze and Bolan watched as they started chewing their own legs off trying to find a route out.

"That should do it. Keep me covered out here until I get inside. I'm going to go find our friends," Bolan said.

"I've got your six," he said.

Bolan dropped the Tavor next to Kowal and pulled out his Desert Eagle as he made his way to the house.

It was time to put an end to the Undead Posse once and for all.

As he ran toward the house, Bolan saw Spook leap out of the shattered window and roll to his feet. The man moved closer to the house, trying to blend into the shadows, but didn't count on being seen. Bolan fired two rounds into the rocks at his feet, kicking up a spray of shrapnel that tore through Spook's clothing and dug into the tender flesh beneath.

Spook shouted in pain, grabbing for his legs, and never even saw Bolan coming. The big American closed the distance and swept the man's feet out from under him, pinning him with the Desert Eagle—an up close and personal view of the big weapon that would make almost any man squirm.

"Where's Crisp?" Bolan demanded.

"An' how should I be knowing? Getting shot at don't make him loyal, does it?"

"You have five seconds to tell me where he is or where he'd go from here, or you're no use to me." Bolan gestured with the Desert Eagle. "In this scenario, useless people die."

A shot split the air behind him. Bolan spun to see the stunned face of a posse member who had been trying to put a machete through his skull. His eyes widened in surprise at the bullet hole in his chest, the machete fell from nerveless fingers and he collapsed in a heap. Spook took advantage of Bolan's distraction and lashed out at his knee.

The soldier bent the knee and went to the ground, preventing what could have been a serious injury, but giving up his position. Spook came up throwing dirt in his face. Bolan turned his head at the last second, protecting his eyes, but caught a punch to his jaw.

He dropped to his side, ears ringing a bit, but managed a quick side kick that caught Spook in the solar plexus. The big man doubled over, gasping for air. Bolan got to his feet, but was no sooner there than he was caught from behind by the Obeah man.

He shoved himself backward, trying to pull away, but the shaman was stronger than he looked, and his hands were like a vise, locked in place over Bolan's chest. He tried again, but the Obeah man didn't budge, so either his strength was magically enhanced or the man was hopped up on drugs of some kind.

"Now it's my turn," Spook snarled, rushing toward him.

"Nope, mine," Kowal said, plowing into the group at full speed.

Everyone crashed to the ground, and Bolan rolled out of the mix, momentarily thankful that he'd thought to get Kowal involved. He took a position and waited as the Obeah man and Spook got to their feet. He wanted them alive for questioning, and just killing them wouldn't get him any closer to Crisp. The two men looked at him, Kowal and each other, then both took off in different directions.

"Take him," Bolan shouted, gesturing after the Obeah man, even as he turned to chase after Spook.

For whatever reason, Spook had run in the direction of the beach and was doing his best to get to where the sand ended and the rocks began. He was a fairly large man, strong, but not incredibly fast. Twenty-five yards shy of the man's apparent goal, Bolan caught up to him, knocking him down from behind. Spook scrambled to get away, clawing at the sand.

Bolan grabbed one flailing foot and yanked him backward. Spook continued to squirm and one random kick caught Bolan square in the crotch. He grunted in pain, dropping to his knees, and Spook chose that moment to stop fighting wildly and start fighting in earnest. He leaped forward, slamming into Bolan, and the two rolled across the sand, punching at each other and looking for an opening to end the battle.

Spook managed to land on top when they stopped rolling and grasped Bolan by the throat, trying to strangle him. Unable to breath, and at a severe position disadvantage, Bolan thrust upward with all his strength, trying to break the man's hold. Somehow, Spook held on, as if he were a leech, and stars began to swim in Bolan's vision. He thrashed again, and this time Spook's grip loosened slightly.

The tiny trickle of air felt wonderful until his opponent tightened his grip once more. Knowing he was out of options, Bolan ignored the hands at his throat and pulled the combat knife from the sheath in his boot. He twisted slightly, then drove the blade between Spook's third and fourth ribs, angling it upward and penetrating his heart.

Spook stiffened in shock, then collapsed on top of him, his hands loosening as he died. Bolan pushed the man off him, pulled out the knife and wiped the blood on the dead man's shirt. Then he stuck it back in his boot.

"I'd have been a lot happier if we'd saved this dispute for after you talked," Bolan said

He turned and ran back down the beach, hoping that Kowal had managed to catch the Obeah man and not kill him. He went up and over a sand dune just in time to see Kowal draw down and put two rounds into the shaman.

Kowal turned as he approach and shook his head. "There

was no way that crazy son of a bitch was going to talk, Cooper."

"How do you know?" he asked.

Kowal pointed to a dark flap of flesh on the sand. "Because when I started to catch up to him, he bit off his own tongue."

"I guess I'd have to agree with you, then," Bolan said.

"I just hope he doesn't come back to life or something. He's got more bones tied into his hair than a graveyard."

"If he does, you can shoot him again," Bolan replied. He knelt and searched through the Obeah man's clothing. "Nothing," he said. On the other side of the house, he could see the flashing lights from the arriving police cars. They wouldn't hesitate to go inside, especially since this had to have been a known posse house. "Let's get up to the house and see what we can find. Maybe we can get something useful before the locals tear the place up."

Disappointed that they'd lost Jacob Crisp once again, Bolan led the way as the wind kicked up off the ocean, sending sand swirling around their feet. They reached the house and headed for the back patio door, but stopped short as several police officers came through.

Bolan quickly held up his CIA credentials and asked to speak to the officer in charge. A short, stocky man in uniform came forward and introduced himself as Sergeant Benson.

They shook hands, and Bolan offered a fairly abbreviated explanation of what had happened. Considering that the Montego Bay Police Department had its hands full simply trying to repair its reputation for scandal, corruption and failure, Benson was only too happy to help in an official CIA investigation. He happily agreed to let Bolan search the residence while he sent his officers scouring the area for hiding posse members and additional evidence.

Bolan and Kowal split up and searched the house. Bolan

opened the door to the master suite and was overwhelmed by the smell of gun cleaning solvent. He flicked on the light switch and immediately saw the source of the smell. Four cases of automatic weapons were opened and in various states of cleaning and stacking throughout the room. He looked at the crates and saw the Russian stamps on the side. Bolan shook his head. Ever since the cold war ended and the upheaval in the Russian government, it's seemed like there was an endless supply of black-market Russian weapons.

Bolan finished his search and met back in the center with Kowal. "Anything?'

"Nah, well, yeah, some drug stashes, but nothing that affects us."

"Damn."

Kowal was searching the living room while Bolan checked the last of the bedrooms when he called out, "Hey, Cooper, you should see this."

Bolan returned to the living room to find Kowal holding a small netbook in his hand. He ran a finger over the touch pad and the screen came to life. The system was still logged on, and Bolan began searching through the files. There weren't many documents on the system, so he began to scroll through the email. One of the messages definitely caught his attention.

There was no sender name or email address, which meant it had been routed through at least one or two blind servers, but the message was direct and to the point:

Crisp: Dock 8, 3AM, Extraction.

Embedded within the email was a map of the various dock areas around Montego Bay.

"That's it, then," Bolan said. "They're going to get Crisp off the island. If he manages to escape, we'll likely never see him again."

Bolan waved Benson over. "Sergeant, can you tell me where this dock is located?"

Benson looked down at the email message and shook his head. "That cannot be right," he said.

"Why?" Bolan asked.

"Because that is not a civilian docking area. The docks are numbered, and that one is for the local coast guard, U.S. Coast Guard and the Navy. Occasionally, when traffic is heavy, they will allow an industrial freighter to use that pier, but no civilian vessels."

"Where is it?"

"Here," he said, pointing out the dock location on the map.

Bolan and Kowal hitched a lift back to their vehicle, where they found Reggie waiting for them.

"Did you get the bad guys?" Reggie asked.

"Some of them," Bolan said.

"The Obeah man?" he asked, sounding genuinely concerned.

"He's dead," Kowal reassured him. "His grave-robbing, spell-casting days are over for good."

"That is good," the boy said. "It would be bad if he could cast curses on us."

"Reggie," Bolan said, putting a hand on his shoulder, "I want you to wait for us here. If I give you some money, can you get yourself a room where we rented the Jet Skis?"

"Yes, but I—"

"No 'buts' this time," he interrupted. Bolan pulled some cash from his wallet and handed it to the kid. "I want you somewhere safe. As soon as we're done, I'll make sure you get home."

Looking a little disgruntled, but clearly calculating how he could keep the money, Reggie nodded. "You're the boss."

"Good," Bolan replied. "And I do mean it. Don't follow us."

Reggie held up the cash and smiled. "I won't. I have other plans." The boy turned and ran in the direction of the resort, and Bolan could only hope he wouldn't spend it on something less than savory.

"Good…I think," he said, then he glanced at his watch and turned to Kowal. "Let's get going. We've still got time to get to Crisp before his ship leaves."

The two men jumped in the car and raced into the early-morning hours.

The docks were lit by orange-colored sodium arc lamps, which left plenty of areas in shadow. The ships groaned and rocked back and forth in their berths as the two men moved along the various stone quays. All of the vessels were either military or commercial ships—not one of them was civilian that Bolan could see. He and Kowal parked the car and got out, moving quickly for Dock 8.

"What are we looking for?" Kowal asked quietly.

"I'd think a boat getting ready to leave," he replied. "Maybe something smaller than these."

"Makes sense," Kowal said, then added after a moment, "though maybe that's too easy. You hear that?" He stopped walking and cupped a hand to his ear.

Bolan nodded. "It's coming closer," he said, as the distinct sound of a helicopter's whirling blades penetrated the early-morning air. It was close to 3:00 a.m. so daylight was at least two and half hours away.

"Let's move," he said, running down the pier that led farther into the bay.

Ahead, a concrete helipad came into view. Bolan scanned

the area and saw Crisp as he broke cover, running to catch his ride to safety

"Take the chopper," Bolan said, sliding to a halt and drawing the Desert Eagle. "Try to back it off!"

He opened fire, but he was still more than two hundred yards out. The powerful handgun was brutally effective, but at that range, its accuracy was poor. The drop rate of the heavy .50-caliber round he used was simply too fast. He kept firing, hoping to convince the helicopter not to land, but it continued its descent and began to swing around.

Kowal didn't bother to open fire but kept moving along the pier, hoping to get close enough for his smaller weapon to make a difference.

Crisp ran for the chopper, and Bolan saw that the side door was open and a gunman was wedged behind a mounted machine gun. The aircraft was a Super Lynx 300—a British navy attack helicopter—but the insignia was U.S. Coast Guard. He hit the deck, yelling for Kowal to do the same, fearing that the entire pier was about to be covered in hot lead, but his voice was drowned out by the high-pitched spin of the blades. Instead, a short burst of fire dropped Crisp in a heap on the pad.

Bolan watched as the chopper immediately reversed course and vanished into the dark sky. He got to his feet and ran to where the posse leader was already being looked at by Kowal, who shook his head.

The soldier knelt next to the dying man, who coughed and tried to roll to his side. Blood leaked from his mouth in thin, bright rivulets. He turned back and caught Bolan's gaze. Crisp was about to die a second time, but Bolan suspected this one would take better than the first.

"Never trust Americans, Agent Cooper. Posse will kill you, but they don't lie to you about it."

"Which Americans?" Bolan asked. "Anders?"

Crisp relaxed back to the ground, his time running out rapidly. Bolan cradled the man's head in his hands.

"Anders, yes," he gasped. "And that damn boatman."

"Boat man?"

"He always say the same thing…*simper paratus*…damn sailor man." The blood gurgled from his mouth and cut off any more information. He jerked once, then died. Bolan looked at Crisp and then at Kowal.

"Semper Paratus," he said. "The Coast Guard?"

"What do they have to do with this mess?" Kowal asked.

"I don't know," Bolan said, "but that chopper had Coast Guard insignia, so I guess we'll find out."

Kowal offered him a hand up, and Bolan took it. The helipad was covered in blood spatters from Crisp. All their efforts for the night had led to more questions than answers—and more dead men than living ones. The Executioner knew that the men responsible for the terrorist attack in the States were still out there. Somewhere.

THE DRIVE BACK to the resort to pick up Reggie was mercifully quiet. Kowal stared out the window at the passing scenery, keeping his thoughts to himself, likely pondered the maze that they seemed to be trapped in. With Crisp dead, Bolan knew that the Undead Posse had been nothing more than a pawn in someone's larger scheme, but he doubted that Anders was the one running the show. He didn't seem the type, nor did he appear to have enough power on his own.

They picked up Reggie just as the sun was peeking over the horizon. The boy appeared in the parking lot before Bolan had even had a chance to shut off the engine. He jumped in the backseat, grinning from ear to ear.

"Glad you're alive, boss," he said, slamming the door shut. "Did you kill him?"

"I didn't," Bolan said, "but he's just as dead. The Undead Posse is out of business, at least for now."

"Good," the boy said. "What next?"

"That's a good question," Kowal said. "Where do you go from here?"

"Back to Kingston," Bolan replied. "I've got to get back to the States as soon as I can."

Kowal nodded. "Unless you think you need me for something else, I suspect I'd best be getting back to the resort." He almost sounded sad.

"Not for any reason I can think of," Bolan said. He put the car into gear and headed back down the road. "You've been a friend," he added. "Thank you."

"My pleasure," Kowal replied. "I've missed it more than I thought I did, and those were some bad people we took care of. I call that a good day's work."

"Me, too," Reggie piped up from the back.

Both men laughed. They drove the rest of the way back to Kingston in companionable silence. Once they arrived, Bolan guided the vehicle to the American Embassy, only to be informed by the guard on duty that Conrad Anders had not reported in, and they'd been unable to locate him thus far. Since the guard didn't even try to hold him for questioning, Bolan assumed that Anders hadn't even bothered to try to continue the farce that he was a diplomatic problem to be deported.

Leaving the embassy, Bolan took Kowal back to his vehicle. "Give me just a minute to make an update call," he said, "then we can wrap up."

"Sure thing," he replied, climbing out and sorting through the gear to repack his and separate it from Bolan's. He gave Reggie the evil eye until the kid got the idea and jumped out to help, then Bolan used his cell phone to contact Hal Brognola.

Despite the early hour, Brognola answered before the first ring had finished. "Striker, what's your status?" he asked.

"Tired," Bolan replied. "You?"

“We’re running in circles,” the big Fed said. “Nobody has any clue at all how the anthrax attack happened or if it’s likely to happen again. And I’m trying to keep a lid on the other girls you found until we know who is behind this, but it’s not easy.”

“I think it’s likely to happen again if we don’t get a handle on it soon,” Bolan said. “But this is a mess of tangled knots and I’m just about at a dead end.”

“Give me the rundown.”

“The Undead Posse is officially out of business, at least until they come up with some new management. Jacob Crisp and his main bodyguard, a man they called Spook, are both dead. So is the Obeah man they were using to cloak the anthrax attacks in superstition and magic.”

“That was fast work. What did you get from Crisp before you took him out?”

“That’s just it, Hal. I can take responsibility, along with Kowal, for Spook and the Obeah man, but someone else took out Crisp.”

“You’re kidding,” Brognola said. “Who?”

“Someone in a Super Lynx 300 helicopter with Coast Guard insignia,” Bolan replied. “I’m guessing whoever his accomplice really is decided that he was too much of a liability or didn’t need him anymore. He didn’t have a clue it was coming, either. They just popped up out of the water and killed him. He thought he was getting rescued.”

“Did you get anything?” Brognola asked.

“He said something about not trusting Americans and specifically mentioned sailors and the Coast Guard motto. Any of that mean anything to you?”

“Not really, but it would make a certain amount of sense. The Coast Guard heavily patrols the area, and they’d have easy access to the ports both there and in the States. One thing doesn’t make sense, though.”

"What's that?" Bolan asked, holding up a finger to Kowal who was looking at him through the window.

"The Coast Guard doesn't use Super Lynx choppers," Brognola said. "Those are foreign. Britain and some of the European countries use them for all kinds of things."

Bolan considered it, but shook his head. "There's no telling at this point. Either way, this whole operation is bigger than just what's going on down here in Jamaica. Maybe they've got someone in the Coast Guard helping out or at least looking the other way."

"Maybe," Brognola said, but doubt registered in his voice. "Or maybe he was just lying to you, Striker."

"I don't think so," Bolan countered. "Crisp considered it a betrayal, which makes me think this was a more active partnership than just look the other way as a ship passes by. You have anyone in your head who would be capable of pulling off something like this?"

"Not offhand," he replied. "But I'll do a little digging and see what I can come up with. What else have you got?"

"Conrad Anders is gone. My guess is that he's already headed back to the States and looking to hook up with whoever is really running this show."

"So what's next?" the big Fed asked. "Are you out of leads?"

"I'm done down here, but I need a flight to Washington, D.C. I want to see if I can track down Anders and maybe have a little chat with him."

"Okay, Striker," Brognola said. "I'll make the arrangements. Anything else?"

"Yeah, two things," Bolan said. "Did you check out this guy Rob Kowal?"

"Yeah, he's the real deal. Great record in the Secret Service and in the Rangers before that. Clean as a whistle. Went private sector a couple of years ago."

"I thought so. He's been solid as a rock down here. I want

to give him your number. I get the sense that this private-security deal he's working might be a little too sedate for him."

"If you're recommending him, Striker, I'll talk with him. The money won't be nearly as good, though. What's the second issue?"

"This kid, Reggie," Bolan said. "He's in it for the money, and I've paid him pretty well, but he doesn't get it. Even without Crisp around, those who are left in the Undead Posse are going to know he helped me. We've been seen by too many people."

"That's kind of a tough sell," Brognola said. "He's just a kid. What do you want me to do with him?"

"He's put his life on the line to help," Bolan said. "If he wants an out, could you pull some strings and maybe get him into protective custody?"

"Maybe," Brognola said. "How important is this to you?"

"I wouldn't ask if it wasn't," Bolan replied. "I'm not in the habit of leaving people in the lurch."

"All right. If he's willing, we'll work it to get him and his family into some kind of witness protection program back here in the States."

"Thanks, Hal," Bolan said. "I'll call you once I'm stateside and know more." He ended the call and got out of the car. Kowal and Reggie were leaning on the hood, chatting quietly.

"Your boss have anything new?" Kowal asked.

"Not a thing," he replied. "He's going to do some digging, but I have to get back to the States. I'm going after Anders."

"Then I guess this is goodbye," Kowal said. He stepped forward and shook Bolan's hand. The soldier took out a slip of paper and wrote Brognola's Justice Department phone number on it, then handed it to Kowal.

"What's this?" he asked.

Bolan grinned. "Just in case you decide that you need

something a little more active than the private-security thing. My contact will be expecting your call."

Kowal smiled in return and nodded. "Thank you."

"What about me?" Reggie chimed. "Do I get a bonus?'

Bolan wrote the information once more and handed it to Reggie.

"You want me to be a secret agent?" the boy asked.

"No, but you do get a bonus if you and your family want it. If you call that man there and give him your name, he can help you out. There are posse members here that will know you helped me, and you won't be safe. That man can get you and your family to safety."

"In America?" Reggie asked. "Really?"

"Really," he replied. "And they'll set you up as citizens. You were a great help Reggie, and I couldn't have gotten this far without you."

"Thanks, boss. Maybe in America someday I'll be your boss, right?"

"I wouldn't be the least bit surprised." He offered the boy his hand, who took it with a serious look on his face. Then, before he could say more, the kid laughed, turned and ran down the road.

"Hope he takes you up on that," Kowal said.

"Me, too," Bolan replied.

"Get in touch if you need something."

"I will," Bolan said. They shook once more, then both men left, each headed for his own destination. Kowal to do some thinking on his future, no doubt, but Bolan needed to find Conrad Anders.

And when he did, Anders was going to tell him everything.

During the long flight from Kingston to Washington, D.C., with a layover eating up even more time in Fort Lauderdale, Bolan had plenty of time to consider the convoluted mess he was dealing with. Someone with a lot more power than Conrad Anders had to be pulling the strings of this operation. Bolan suspected that Anders had been the point man in Jamaica, and it was his idea to use the Undead Posse to gather bodies for shipping the biological weapons, using local superstitions as cover for the real purpose.

But the helicopter with Coast Guard insignia pointed to help from outside Jamaica. It was certainly possible, given Brognola's information that the Coast Guard didn't actually use that kind of chopper, that someone was simply trying to point him in the wrong direction. Either way, in order to find out more, he was going to have to question Anders personally.

After the layover, Bolan was seated next to a young man who pored over a stack of books during the flight—everything from navigation to military history, and even one on ship design. He wasn't in uniform, but he had a military-style haircut and the bearing of someone in the service. "A little light reading?" Bolan asked.

"I'm studying for the Service Wide Exam," he said. "I didn't make the promotion list last time, so I really need to score high this time."

"The Service Wide Exam?" Bolan asked.

"Sorry," he said. "I figured you probably knew. You look like you're in the service or something. It's a test we take to make rank in the Coast Guard. You can't promote unless you do well."

"I didn't know that," Bolan said, "but my familiarity with the Coast Guard is limited." Bolan watched the young man for another minute, as he tried to pin everything down in his head.

"So are you stationed here in Florida?" he asked.

"No, I was down visiting a couple of buddies who are docked here right now, and I'm sure glad it's not my boat. The skipper is a little mental, from what they tell me. I'm on my way back to Virginia, where at least the skipper makes sense."

"Mental, huh? Why's that?"

The young man shrugged. "Who knows, really? You'd be surprised how much authority gets into some people's heads. Anyways, I guess their orders change a lot here, and he really bites the crew's head off when things don't go right. That boat is his own little fiefdom."

"Hmm... That's interesting."

"Well, you know how it is, follow orders and keep your head down, and maybe the next duty station will be better."

"There's always someplace better," Bolan said. "Good luck with your test."

"Thanks," he replied, then turned back to his books.

A little while later, the plane touched down and Bolan rebooted his smartphone. There was a message waiting from Brognola, which included a map of the D.C. area and a notation that Anders had been spotted near Capitol Building. A car and equipment waited for him in the parking ramp.

With no luggage to collect, Bolan got the key from a parking attendant, as instructed, got into the vehicle he was shown to and was quickly on his way out of the airport parking garage. He headed toward the center of Washington, D.C. While he'd been here any number of times, the traffic never failed to remind him of being in a firefight. Everyone moved as fast as they could, but without any real direction or purpose, you were just as likely to get hit by the guy next to you as you were someone that was a half mile down the road.

Looking for his exit, Bolan switched lanes and saw a vehicle switch behind him, too. It was possible, even probable, that it was mere coincidence, but something told him that he had a new friend. He switched lanes twice more, and both times the vehicle moved with him.

He exited the highway, going to surface streets, then turned onto Dupont Circle. The car continued to tail him as he made his way to Capitol Hill. The streets were thronged with commuters getting off work, tourists trying to get their last pictures in and any number of taxis and tour buses. The odds of the same vehicle coincidentally being on the same route were fairly small. The driver was working too hard to stay close to Bolan.

He made a last turn and spotted Anders getting into a sedan. Maneuvering to catch up, he switched lanes in a hurry, but that was when his newfound shadow decided to make his move. Accelerating quickly, the vehicle behind him rammed into his bumper, then whipped around to get in front of him.

Bolan ignored the vehicle, trying to turn around to get back to where Anders had been, but a second car appeared behind him, the windows went down and the guns came out.

"The Capitol Police are about to have a very bad day," Bolan muttered, swerving even as the gunmen opened fire.

Bolan slammed on his brakes, and the black sedan slammed into his back bumper. In his rearview mirror, he could see the driver frantically changing gears. The soldier pulled forward about ten feet, then jammed the transmission into Reverse, crashing into the vehicle behind him hard enough to set off the driver's air bag and fill the passenger compartment with silvery-gray powder.

With the driver down, his passenger staggered out of the car, trying to raise his semiauto pistol once more. Bolan threw open his own door and rolled, then came up firing the Desert Eagle. In the confined urban environment, the weapon was as intimidating as a cannon when it went off, and the shots echoed off nearby buildings. The first round was slightly off the mark, but the next one took the shooter in the chest, blowing him out of his shoes and into the gutter.

Sirens began to wail nearby, and Bolan knew that if the Capitol Police showed up, there'd be no getting out of the situation without a major hassle. They weren't known for their appreciation for gunfire anywhere near the Capitol Building, let alone the White House.

He ran to the other car and looked inside, but it was fairly clean. The driver was starting to come around, and the sirens were getting closer. On the dash was a portable GPS, which he grabbed, then he ran back into his own vehicle. He took off down the street and was turning the corner just as law enforcement arrived on the scene on the opposite block.

Fortunately, he knew that it would take them a while to piece everything together, review witness statements and likely even look at camera footage. There were a lot of surveillance cameras in the D.C. area, so it wasn't out of the question that the whole thing had been videotaped.

He kept driving as he pulled out his cell phone and called up Brognola.

"Striker, are you in D.C.?"

"I am," he replied, "and I've already created a hell of a mess that I don't have time to clean up. I'm going to need some help with the locals."

Bolan could envision the big Fed shaking his head. "I'm almost afraid to ask what's happened," he said, "but tell me anyway."

Following the coordinates in the GPS while he drove, Bolan filled in Brognola, all the while getting closer to Anders, whose vehicle he hoped was the one that the GPS was tracking.

THE STREETS OF D.C. near the Vietnam Memorial were crowded, and parking appeared to be out of the question until Bolan noticed a spot reserved for police vehicles and pulled in. He jumped out of the car and sprinted across the grass toward the memorial. The Wall itself couldn't be seen from the road, situated as it was at the base of several small hills that gave the park a larger, almost isolated feeling in the middle of what was actually a busy plaza. He made his way to a small tree line where he could see the Wall, as well as the two entrance walks that led to it. Anders had parked his car in this area, and unless he'd gone inside a building, Bolan was going to have to trust his instinct that said the man was here somewhere. It was a good place for a meet.

The Wall was a beautiful memorial of black granite and a list of names that would make any serviceman shiver. That had been a difficult war, a terrible time in America's history, and while a memorial would never make everything right, this one came as close as Bolan thought those soldiers would ever get.

He scanned the area carefully and finally spotted Anders sitting on a bench. While he was obviously trying to look inconspicuous, every time a new person entered the area, he whipped his head around to examine the person closely. There were three other people in the immediate area—two in uniform and one woman, pushing a stroller. The uniformed men walked away just as another uniformed man walked down the sloping walkway.

Anders stood to greet him, and the two men sat down to talk. The man looked vaguely familiar, but Bolan couldn't place him. He used his smartphone to snap a photo, then used the recognition software built into it to try for a match. The database wasn't anywhere close to what Stony Man Farm had available, but it held commonly known people, as well as the most recent data on known criminal types. It quickly came back with a hit. The man was the commandant of the United States Coast Guard, James Bailey.

"This isn't good," he said to himself. He took another photo of the two men talking, then sent the images off to Brognola, along with a quick text message. If things went wrong or something happened to him, someone else needed to know of Bailey's involvement.

They spoke for several minutes, and it was clear to Bolan, despite not being able to hear the conversation, that Anders was on the edge of full-blown panic. His gestures became more and more dramatic, culminating when they got to their feet and Anders grabbed Bailey by the arm. Bailey stopped then and simply stared at the embassy man, who dropped his hand. The commandant then nodded once, turned and walked away. It appeared as though Anders wanted to say something more, but his shoulders sagged. He turned and moved in the opposite direction, heading back to where he'd parked his car.

BOLAN RETURNED to his own vehicle, flashed his CIA credentials at the traffic cop writing out a ticket and climbed in. He pulled out into traffic and found that he was only three or four cars behind Anders. A confrontation near the Vietnam War Memorial wasn't exactly low-key, but he could follow him long enough to find a better place to get what he needed out of the man. Preferably somewhere very private.

Anders headed toward the outskirts of the city, then cut south along the shoreline. The traffic was starting to thin out, and Bolan had to drop back a fair distance. Still, he was close enough to see that all of the shipyards in this area were secured behind high fences. Warehouses stood in neat rows, with pallets and large crates stacked along the open areas, most of them waiting for inspections and customs to finish their work.

Anders pulled in at the security gate and stopped, while Bolan continued driving past, looking for a place where he could park and examine the layout of the area more carefully. Short of a frontal assault on the gate, he needed to find a less destructive and noisy way inside. A half mile down the road, he found what he needed: a parking lot for dockworkers. He pulled in, parked his vehicle, then headed back on foot to the shipyard that Anders had now disappeared into.

The perimeter was fenced off completely, but there was space between the area Anders had entered and the next property. Heavily shadowed, it would work as cover until Bolan could get over the fence and inside to explore. He took a running start at the chain-link fence, and then was up and over, silently thankful that whoever had designed the security had not opted for concertina wire or electrical fencing.

He landed on the other side and started to turn when he heard the sound of gravel crunching beneath a boot. Bolan spun, but it was too late. The Taser fired and the dart raced forward, hitting him in the chest.

Electricity coursed through his body and he went over backward, hitting the fence on the way down.

17

Bolan hit the ground, rolled and got lucky.

The Taser dart slipped loose from his clothes and the electricity stopped. He climbed slowly to his feet and saw that a security guard had caught him coming over the fence. The sentry dropped the Taser handle to the ground and clawed for the extendable baton at his belt.

"You don't want to do that," Bolan said, trying to shake off the effects of the electrical current that had just pulsed through his body. It felt as if he'd been stung by bees *under* his skin. He shook his arms to get the blood flowing and moved closer to the guard.

"Then don't you move, mister," the guard said. He snapped his wrist and the baton extended a full twenty inches in length. It was made of steel and could easily break bones or knock someone senseless.

"I'm afraid I don't have much choice," Bolan replied. "I have work to do."

"Yeah, well, me, too," he said. "This is my job, so I gotta hold you here." He reached for the microphone clipped to his shoulder.

Bolan saw that the man was in his early twenties, just a

kid really, trying to do his job. Wispy blond hair was sneaking out from beneath his cap, and his hand was shaking as he reached for the microphone. "Don't do it, kid," he said. "I'll have to stop you, and it won't be pleasant."

"Just shut up, mister, and don't move," he said, grabbing for the mike.

Bolan shot forward. Reaching out with his left arm and catching the underside of the guard's right, he found the pressure point inside the elbow and squeezed. At the same time, he twisted slightly and drove his right fist into the man's solar plexus.

The air left the sentry's lungs with a faint wooshing sound, but the sound that truly mattered to Bolan was the one of the baton hitting the ground. He stepped closer to the guard, twisted underneath the man and took the arm with him, locking it behind his back.

"Don't struggle, kid," he said, reaching forward to grasp him beneath the chin. "It only gets worse from here."

The guard either didn't believe him, didn't know better or simply felt he didn't have a choice, because he began to thrash violently. He twisted and turned, despite the added pressure Bolan applied to his right arm, then somehow managed to wriggle free.

The guard lashed out with a punch that clipped Bolan on the chin, hard enough to pop his head back slightly.

"All right," Bolan said, closing fast. "That's enough of that."

The guard threw wild punches, which Bolan ducked under, and then he got inside, driving an uppercut into the guard's jaw with bone-crunching force. He followed it with a left into the body, and the young man began to fold. "One more for the road," Bolan said, throwing his last punch in tight, right behind the guard's left ear.

He went down in a heap, unconscious. Bolan rubbed his jaw and shook his head ruefully. "You were more than game," he said softly, "but they're not paying you enough to die." He hooked his hands in the guard's armpits and dragged him behind a tall stack of pallets, then he used the handcuffs on his utility belt to shackle him to the fence.

Removing the microphone from the guard's rig and the cell phone from his belt, Bolan thought it would be at least a half hour, maybe longer, before anyone found the man, who was still blissfully unaware of his current predicament. He'd have to hope that Anders was still here and he'd have time to deal with him before the whole shipyard was swarming with angry security guards.

He looked down once more at the unconscious man. If they were all scrappers like this one, he'd have his hands full. Turning away, Bolan moved deeper into the shipyard.

BOLAN FOUND Anders's car parked in front of a warehouse on the far end of the shipyard. The vehicle was empty, but at least it was still there. He found a door on the side of the building and used it, slipping inside.

It was dark and quiet, with stacks of crates that made him feel like a rat getting ready to negotiate a maze. Bolan walked down a line of crates, moving toward the center of the warehouse floor. From there, his intention was to work his way to the other side of the building and search the offices.

Reaching the center, he saw that there was a solitary crate by itself, and the lid was dislodged. He paused, not liking the setup at all. Bolan pulled a small, extendable mirror from the kit he carried inside his vest. The device held a miniature camera behind the glass that transmitted directly to his handheld computer. He slipped the mirror inside the small crack and rocked it back and forth, watching on his handheld computer for the image of what was inside the crate.

He realized that what he was looking at was a bomb of

some kind. He could see the plastique, but not the device itself. He removed the mirror, then transmitted the images to Brognola at the Justice Department.

A moment later, his handheld computer flashed, signaling an incoming call. "Did you get those, Hal?" he asked, trying to keep his voice down.

"Yeah, I got it. I want to get one of our bomb guys on it. Stand by."

The connection went silent, and Bolan cursed softly to himself. He couldn't stand here trying to disarm a bomb if Anders was still in the building. On the other hand, it seemed likely that this had been left as a clumsy, though deadly trap for him, so Anders was probably long gone.

The connection beeped and a voice came on the line. "Mr. Cooper, my name is Jeffrey. I'm going to walk you through disarming this bomb, since there's no way we can get a bomb squad to you within the time frame on the timer."

"I didn't see a timer," he replied. "I've disarmed a few lid bombs over the years, and they're usually just pull and play."

"We have about fifteen minutes, sir," Jeffrey said. His voice was irritatingly calm.

"How do you know there's fifteen minutes?" Bolan said.

"Image enhancement," he replied. "I'm flashing it to you now."

Bolan looked at the screen of his handheld computer and sure enough, there was a timer, but it was incredibly small and difficult to see unless the image had been enlarged.

"So not a simple lid bomb," he said. "Okay, Jeffrey, it's your show."

"Push the lid halfway open," he replied. "If you go all of the way, then you'll set off the bomb. As you push back the lid, the tension on the trip wires will increase, so watch them carefully."

Bolan carefully slid the lid and looked inside the case.

The mechanism sat on top of four small bricks of plastique. Wires ran from each brick into the bomb trigger. Beneath the trigger was the timing device, still counting down. Bolan used the camera from his handheld computer and gave Jeffrey another view.

"All right, now what?" Bolan asked.

"It's fairly simple. Just clip the blue wires that lead to each brick. The timer will continue to count down, but nothing will happen when the clock reaches zero."

"Cutting the wires won't stop the clock?" he asked.

"Only in the movies, sir," Jeffrey replied. "The timer is run on a battery, and we don't really care what it says so long as the wires aren't attached to the things that go boom."

"Funny, Jeffrey. You've got a real sense of humor there," he replied. Bolan pulled out his multitool and opened the wire cutters. He had to stretch to reach the first wire, and he jostled the lid.

He dropped the multitool as if it were a poisonous snake and quickly rebalanced the crate lid. While he'd done this numerous times in the past, it didn't change the fact that one slip would end his life and probably blow up the entire warehouse.

He reached toward the ground for the multitool. It had slipped between the crates. Bolan grabbed the tool and started to stand when he noticed that the bottom of the crate had what appeared to be a separate compartment of some kind.

He grabbed the tiny mirror once more and slid it into the gap. The images came back on the screen of his handheld computer and he took a deep breath. There were three canisters underneath, each marked with the symbol for biohazard across the bottom. Bolan flashed the images across the connection to Jeffrey.

"Are those connected to the device on top?" he asked.

"I'm not one hundred percent certain," Jeffrey said. "It's

possible that there are wires underneath the plastique, as well."

"Possible?" Bolan asked. "Isn't this something we sort of need to know for sure?"

"It's possible," Jeffrey admitted, "but not probable. The configuration is pretty crude. My best guess is that it's a secondary device. Cut the wires on the first, and then we'll move it away and see what we're dealing with."

Brognola came on the line. "Striker, I've notified the bomb squad and the CDC. They're on their way, but it's going to take some time."

"Perfect," Bolan said, reaching back into the case. He hesitated for the barest second before clipping the wires. Once they were clipped, he said, "Okay, Jeffrey, what next?"

"Lift the plastique away from the timer and the trigger very carefully and look underneath. If there are no wires connected to the bricks, you can lift it out."

Bolan gingerly lifted up the small bricks and peered underneath.

"Nothing," he said.

"Go ahead and remove them," Jeffrey replied. "Just be gentle with the timer."

Bolan did as he was instructed, revealing the canisters below, and a completely separate trigger mechanism, though this one didn't have a timer of any kind. He watched the timer on the plastique tick down to zero. There was an almost inaudible click as the timer tried to activate and then nothing. Bolan let out the breath he hadn't known he was holding.

"Where does that leave us?" Bolan asked, looking at the containers still in the crate.

"Most likely, there's either an internal trigger or some kind of pressure switch on the canisters. Leave them for the bomb squad."

"Sounds like a fine idea," he said. "Hal, are you still on the line?"

"Go ahead, Striker," came Brognola's familiar voice.

"All right, Hal, I'm going to leave this one in the capable hands of the professionals, but I think we need to lock down the warehouses here. I don't trust that this is the only crate of this stuff."

"Agreed."

"I also think Anders knew I'd find this crate. He wasn't worried about the bomb going off. That would have been a bonus. I think he was counting on my missing the stuff in the bottom and then taking out a whole bunch of cops and rescue workers with whatever nasty bug is in those containers."

"That's my read on it, as well. One of the oldest plays in the book, and it still works. These guys are getting out of control, but I need something more on Bailey."

"What do you mean?"

"Striker, he's way up in the food chain. Practically at the same level as the Joint Chiefs. And he's as clean as a whistle. I haven't been able to dig up anything on him, and just meeting up with Anders, even now, isn't nearly enough to have him picked up. He'll say it's simply a matter of an unfortunate acquaintance."

Bolan knew Brognola was right, but that didn't mean he had to like it. "Well, Anders is still out there somewhere, and he knows that we're onto him. That means Bailey does, too."

"You're going to have to move fast to get the evidence we need before he cleans up his tracks and vanishes."

Bolan considered the situation for a minute, then said, "I'll get what you need, Hal. In fact, I'm on my way as soon as the police arrive. I just need to make a phone call first."

"Good work on this bomb, Striker," Brognola said. "And good luck."

Bolan broke the connection and schooled himself to patience until the police showed up. As soon as he heard the sirens in the distance, he slipped out of the back of the warehouse and headed for his car.

The timer on the bomb may have been deactivated, but the one in his head telling him that Anders and Bailey were about to go on the run was ticking faster than ever.

Sitting at a stoplight on his way back into the city, Bolan sent Kowal a text message and waited for the phone to ring. He needed people that he could trust in Washington, D.C., and that would be difficult enough, but he also needed to find decent people who could act without official orders from the chain of command. That was going to be a tall order, indeed.

Kowal's number lit up the screen of his handheld computer as the call came in.

"Rob, thanks for calling me right back," Bolan answered

"No problem," he said. "Have you caught the bastards yet?"

"Not yet," he admitted. "I've run into some complications."

"A mission without complications isn't going right," Kowal said. "How can I help?"

"Anders gave me the slip again, but he did lead me to the mastermind, a man very high up in the military food chain. In order to bring him down, I'm going to need hard evidence. Do you have anyone who might be able to lend me a hand with intelligence on what's going on locally?"

"That's a complication, all right," he said. "D.C. is a different kettle of fish, and fighting there is more finesse than muscle. I was thinking of you, so I put in a call to a friend of mine early this morning. Name's Mike Peterson. I'm texting you the number. Give him a call, and maybe you can get pointed in the right direction."

"Thanks, Rob. I appreciate the assist."

"Don't mention it," he said. "Just get the bastards."

Bolan hung up and glanced at the text message Kowal had sent. He highlighted the number and hit the Send button.

The line rang twice then a woman's voice answered crisply, "Peterson."

A bit surprised, Bolan said, "I'm sorry, I was trying to reach Mike Peterson."

"This is Mike Peterson, though only one person has called me that today, and he's working in Jamaica. You must be Matt Cooper," she said.

"I am," he said. "I guess I wasn't—"

"Expecting a woman?" she asked. "I'm not surprised. Rob's got a strange sense of humor. How can I help you, Mr. Cooper?"

"You can start by telling me who you are. All Rob said was that you might be able to help me."

"A cautious man," she replied, laughing softly. "I like that."

Wishing he had more time for flirtatious banter to answer the sexy voice on the other line, but knowing he didn't, he simply said, "It's a personal trademark, but I still need to know."

"Fair enough," she said. "I work for the Secret Service, Mr. Cooper, as the D.C. scheduling master. I'm also Rob's ex-girlfriend, but I don't hold a grudge. We parted amicably."

"Scheduling master, huh?"

"Yes. It's my job to make sure that there are Secret Service agents in the right places at the right time, all the time."

"That must be a difficult job," Bolan said.

"You've got no idea," she replied. "Now, do you want my help or not?"

It was a risk, Bolan knew, but his choices were limited. "I do," he said. "Please."

"Great, how can I help?" she asked.

"I need to know where Coast Guard Commandant James Bailey is going to be today. Can you find that out?"

"He's not one of our protectees," she said. "Hold on a minute."

In the background, he could hear her tapping away on a keyboard. "Do I want to know why—scratch that—I don't want to know why. If Rob says you're one of the good guys, then I'll accept that, but if you're up to bad business, I'll hunt you down myself, understood?"

"Yes, ma'am," Bolan replied. "Understood."

"Okay, then," she replied, "and don't call me ma'am. Makes it sound like I'm a hundred and twelve."

"I'm sure you're not," he said.

"I'm not," she said. "Not even close. I've got what you're looking for. The Joint Chiefs are meeting at the Pentagon today. He's scheduled to be there for a meeting with them in about an hour. I can send you the specifics, but you'll have to have some pretty good credentials to get inside. The meeting isn't going to happen where the tourists can just walk by and wave hello."

"The good meetings never are," Bolan admitted. "Just send me the information and I'll do the rest."

"On its way to you now, Mr. Cooper. And good luck with whatever you're doing."

"Thank you, Mike," he said. "You've been a big help."

"And you owe me dinner the next time you're in town," she said.

"It's a deal," he replied, then cut the connection and turned his attention back to his driving. The agent could obviously be a pleasant distraction, and that was the one thing he didn't need at the moment.

BOLAN PARKED in the Pentagon's south parking lot, then scrolled through the information Peterson had sent to his handheld computer. If he was going to get inside in time to find Bailey, he needed to move quickly. He left the vehicle and crossed the parking lot, then marched through the large columns at the main entrance.

In a lot of ways, the Pentagon looked like most modern-day courthouses—polished tile floors, signs guiding people to a different floor or ring of the building and security guards everywhere you turned. But first, there was the rather significant security checkpoint and the metal detectors. Five rows of security were waiting, two specifically for employees and the other three for visitors.

Flashing his CIA credentials to the young officer on duty, he opened his jacket to show the Desert Eagle. The young man's eyes widened a bit at the big gun, but he waved for him to move through the law-enforcement side of the metal detector.

"Agent Cooper," the young lieutenant said, stopping him short. "I've been instructed to send you to a quick security briefing with Commander Simms. Please wait for him in the conference room there." He pointed to a small room with a glass door.

"I wasn't advised..." he began, but the young officer just gestured for him to keep moving. Not knowing what to expect, he entered the room. A moment later, an older naval officer entered the room and shut the door behind him.

"I don't really need a security briefing, Commander," Bolan began.

Commander Simms held up his hand. "Please, Agent

Cooper. Mike Peterson got in touch and asked me to lend you a hand. May I see your handheld?"

Bolan handed him the electronic device. "She's right on top of things, isn't she?" he asked.

"One of the best," Simms replied, tapping away at the various options on the screen. "There are a lot of people who wish she was still in the field, instead of driving a desk, but that was her choice."

"She was a field agent?" Bolan asked, surprised. "For the Secret Service?"

"No," he said. "Foreign operative for the CIA. She got made in Iran and spent six months being interrogated before they managed to get her out."

"They don't play nice over there. I'm surprised she's alive," Bolan said.

"If you knew her, you wouldn't be," he said. "From what I've heard, the Iranians were sort of glad to let her go. She plays rough."

"Interesting," Bolan said, filing the information away. One never knew when that kind of person would come in handy.

Simms stopped tapping on the handheld computer's screen. "What I'm about to give you, Agent Cooper, is classified top secret, but the Carsons are very dear to us here and if there *is* a traitor in our midst, I want to do everything possible to help you catch him."

He punched up a map on the handheld computer. "This is a map that details all of the access points for the Pentagon. It's an encrypted file that will delete itself in one hour."

"That's fair," Bolan said.

"You're standing here," he continued, pointing to the screen, "on the E ring. Admiral Bailey is at a meeting on the fourth floor, A ring, in suite 405. He maintains a site office right next door."

"Thank you," Bolan said, meaning it. "This helps a lot."

"Also, it's worth noting that Admiral Bailey added someone to the security list today, a man named Conrad Anders. According to his file, he's the intelligence officer for the U.S. Embassy in Jamaica. Does that mean anything to you?"

"He's here?" Bolan asked, hardly believing his luck. He'd assumed that Anders had already hightailed it out of D.C.

Simms nodded. "He came through about fifteen minutes ago."

"That's excellent news," he said. "Where do you recommend I enter?"

"You can get to him from the main-ring entrance, but I'd suggest you enter through here," he said, pointing to the map once again.

Bolan looked at where Simms was pointing on the map. It looked like a solid wall.

"What am I missing?" he asked.

"When the Pentagon was originally built, they were in a hurry," Simms explained. "Quite often the builders were working ahead of the plan itself. There are several hidden rooms and also exits that are not common knowledge. As a matter of fact, only a handful of people who work here are aware that any of them exist at all. When they did the renovations they sealed up some of them, but used others as secret passages to be able to get to different sections of the Pentagon and also as emergency exits."

"Convenient," Bolan said. "So how do I get in?"

"Simple, this wall is special because it hides an access hallway. Its purpose is for escape if ever one of the Secret Service protectees were here and the facility was attacked or security compromised. When you get close to the wall, press the Send button on your handheld. I've programmed it to emit the signal that will allow you to push open the fake wall. That corridor is quiet for the most part, but you need to make certain that you're not seen."

"I will," he said. "Then where?"

"Once you're inside, you'll see a small ladder on the wall. You can use it to access the crawl space above the rooms in that area. It's small, but you can use the space to drop into any of the offices on that wedge of the ring."

"I got it," Bolan said, putting the handheld computer back on his belt.

"And, Agent Cooper," Simms said, "you already know that if security is made aware of your presence in those areas, we will have no choice but to place you under arrest. But once you have what you need, I can reach any point in this building in seven minutes. Send me a message and I'll be there if you need assistance."

"I don't intend on being seen," Bolan replied, "but all your help is deeply appreciated. You must trust Mike with your life."

"She's one of the good guys," he said. "And if she's vouched for you, then I'll back her play. Just don't make either one of us sorry, Agent Cooper. She has friends in high places."

"So do I, but you won't be sorry," he said. "You have my word."

"Then get going," Simms replied. "There's no telling how long Bailey and Anders will stay put, and it's a big building."

Bolan nodded his thanks, then slipped out of the room and into the corridor. As he made his way through the hallways he marveled at the small city within a building. There were stores, banking, a post office and even a barbershop. He looked down at the map on his handheld computer and realized that if you didn't understand how the building was put together you could wander around for a month and not go anywhere.

He quickly made his way to the A ring, then started down the hallway that held the secret passage. Two airmen were leaning against the wall talking. Bolan walked past and found a men's room down the hall, which he entered, then waited a couple of minutes and came back out.

The two airmen were still standing there, chatting quietly. He walked back to the airmen and stared at them.

"Something you need, sir?" one asked.

"No, but I was in uniform once, and I just thought I'd warn you. I just came out of a briefing and the colonel is on the warpath. You may not want to be lounging in the hallway when he comes by."

Their eyes opened wide, and they were both in a hurry to be elsewhere. Bolan smiled as they rounded the corner. Fresh recruits—he didn't even have to give a name to the colonel. Any angry colonel would strike the fear of God into the boots.

Bolan took the opportunity to press Send on his handheld computer. A small section of wall opened between two display cases. The Executioner ducked inside and secured the entrance. The cubby-size hole opened up into a larger area with the ladder that Simms had described. The small room was lit with the same floodlights that would come on if power was interrupted. It allowed Bolan to see the details of the room, but not every corner.

He scaled the rungs and then crawled along the passage. There were vents every five to ten feet that looked into different rooms. Bolan continued forward until the map showed him to be just above Bailey's office. There was a ceiling vent that actually looked down into the room, which was quite a bit smaller than Bolan would've expected for someone of Bailey's rank. There were no pictures on his desk, awards on his wall, or even any of the typical nautical memorabilia he would have expected to see for a man that had spent his life serving on the sea. Perhaps the office was simply a temporary space he used when he was here, but it showed little character and made Bolan think the man had already started packing his stuff.

Below, the office door opened and Bailey and Anders walked in. For once on this mission, Lady Luck had smiled on him. Apparently, her name was Mike.

He remained still as the two men began to talk.

To Bolan's critical gaze, Anders looked like a lion in a very small cage.

"You need to calm down," Bailey said, taking a seat behind the desk as Anders paced. "You look like a fish dangling from a line with the way you're dancing around. There's nothing to worry about. Cooper will be taken care of, and there's nothing that ties me to the shipments."

"Oh, well, goody for you," Anders snapped. "I'm glad that it's only my ass on the line, Bailey. What a big relief." He turned toward the older man and jabbed a finger in his direction. "I won't be hanged for treason! They aren't going to get me."

"Oh, for God's sake, man! They don't hang people anymore." Bailey waved a hand in dismissal. "Listen, I have a boat standing by if we need it, but I'm almost certain it won't be necessary. Besides, everything goes back to the Jamaican thugs. Unless you haven't done your job, that's where the trail stops. What we really need to do is get the last load distributed. All of this work will have been for nothing if we don't get the message out. The situation at the docks didn't work out, and the whole point of everything we've done is to demonstrate to the administration how vulnerable our shores really are."

"So long as Cooper's around, I don't feel like our shores are all that vulnerable. The man's like a machine."

"Bullshit," Bailey said. "He's just a man. You have to get the last of it delivered, Anders. We'll get Cooper taken care of. Understand?"

"Fine," Anders said. "I understand perfectly. Just remember that we're in this together. If I go down, you go down with me. No one will believe that I was able to pull this off on my own."

Bailey offered him an amused look and said, "Of course. Let's just get it done."

Anders stomped out the door with Bailey behind him.

Bolan pulled out his handheld computer and sent a text message to Simms: URGENT! GPS TAG BAILEY'S CAR AND ROUTE THE SIGNAL TO ME. Slipping back out of his hiding spot, Bolan got back into the hallway, then slipped around the corner into Bailey's office. For a secure building, the door lock was relatively basic and it took him only a moment to pick it.

He entered, shutting the door behind him, and rifled through the desk. There were three files in the drawer that caught his attention. Each one had an OPS designation, followed by a place name—Montego, Keys and D.C. He flipped through the D.C. file first and saw three possible targets, though they were labeled Recruiting Opportunities. Since one of them was Senator Carson, Bolan assumed it was Bailey's own sick method of motivation. He looked a little more carefully at the D.C. targets. All of the remaining so-called opportunities called for immediate action.

He grabbed the files and ran out the door, speed-dialing Brognola as he went.

The rings ended as the line on the other end came to life. Bolan didn't wait for greetings.

"Hal, we've got a problem."

"Break it down for me," he replied, also skipping the niceties

Bolan quickly explained that there were three targets that Bailey had identified for an attack, and all of them were slated to happen on this day. The idea appeared to be to overwhelm the emergency services available to the city and cause enough devastation to make Bailey's point about coastal vulnerabilities in spades.

Seeing Simms up ahead, he waved a quick high sign to the man, who led him through security without slowing him.

"Hal, we need to get these places evacuated," Bolan said.

"Give me the locations again," Brognola said, typing furiously in the background. "I'll get things moving."

Bolan looked at the map inside the folder once more as he made his way through the Pentagon parking lot. With three potential targets and a limited window, it was going to be difficult to secure each of the scenes in time to prevent a major disaster.

"The Washington Monument, the Smithsonian and the Library of Congress," Bolan said.

"I can get things going, and they can start evacuations now, but it would help to know more, Striker. They didn't even specify which Smithsonian building, and that's not a small place. It could take a long time to get every building cleared."

"I know, Hal, but it's the best I've got right now," he said, starting the car and putting it into gear.

"Track them and hopefully they will lead you to the site. If they are just setting things up, we'll be able to intercept them before anything serious happens. If not, then you'll need to detain them and get the information."

"I'm on my way." He disconnected the call and pulled out of the parking lot, accelerating quickly. The small blip on his GPS screen showed Anders and Bailey turning onto

Constitution Avenue. Bolan changed directions and plotted to intercept them near the Library of Congress.

The cars seemed to be moving at a snail's pace, and if he didn't know better, Bolan would've sworn there was some sort of conspiracy at work. He tried to maneuver through the traffic for a better position, but the problem wasn't the lane he was in. All the lanes were crowded as the entire area was filled with tourists slowing and trying to take cell-phone pictures of the various sights while they drove.

Just as he was preparing to switch lanes once more, a gunshot blasted out behind him, shattering the glass of the back windshield. Bolan lowered himself over the steering wheel as two more shots pelted the car. He glanced in the rearview mirror and saw that two vehicles had managed to get in behind him.

The first of them, a large black SUV, sped up and rammed into his bumper with enough force to actually require him to fight the steering wheel, but his efforts were useless. The much larger vehicle was pushing him into the oncoming traffic. Bolan pulled his Desert Eagle and fired two quick shots over his shoulder, and one smashed through the windshield of the SUV.

He wasn't certain if the driver was hit or not, but it didn't matter as the SUV careened into the oncoming lane and collided with a large garbage truck. It spun sideways, was hit a second time and came to rest upside down, with the engine still revving.

The driver of the second vehicle, a tricked-out blue Mustang, didn't want to hang around and swerved around Bolan, trying to speed away.

"Oh, no, you don't," he said, stomping on the gas. It was his turn to shove a vehicle around. He rammed into the rear of the Mustang, crushing the bumper with his larger sedan. The passenger turned in his seat and started shooting wildly, starring the front windshield of Bolan's car. The soldier tried to stay low, using the dash for cover, even as he fired his own rounds at the speeding Mustang. Horns honked and other drivers yelled obscenities as they wove in and out of dangerously close pedestrian and vehicle traffic.

The Mustang swerved over two lanes, narrowly missing a woman pushing a stroller, then hit the brakes, trying to use a city tour bus as cover. Bolan began to slow, contemplating his next move when the Mustang slammed on its brakes, tires squealing, and then turned down a small side street.

Spinning the wheel, Bolan fell in behind them as they cruised back onto 12th Street and headed toward the Washington Marina. The streets widened out in this area, and the Mustang began to pull away.

Seeing that they'd have to make a turn to stay on the road, Bolan floored the accelerator. The mustang tried to skid around the corner, and rather than turn, he simply kept going straight and T-boned the car. Bolan kept his foot on the accelerator, pushing it closer to the Marina, until it smashed up against a concrete piling marking off the parking lot. With both sides of the vehicle crushed, the men inside were effectively trapped.

Bolan jumped out of his car and ran to the side of the Mustang. The driver was either unconscious or dead, his head lolling against his shoulder and blood on his face. The passenger, on the other hand, was trying to escape through the shattered window. Bolan helped him finish his self-extrication by grabbing the man's shirt, yanking him through the window and slamming him to the hard concrete of the parking lot. The Undead Posse tattoo emblazoned on his arm answered most of the questions that Bolan had on the tip of his tongue. Blood oozed from cuts on his arms and legs. The awkward angle of his wrist guaranteed a fracture.

"Where is the next attack?" Bolan demanded.

The posse member spit blood along with a jagged tooth on the ground in front of him. "I won't be tellin' you nothin', blood clot. You already out of time anyway, big man." He tried to sit up.

Bolan kicked him in the chest, knocking him onto his back, and planted a boot on his sternum. Pulling the Desert Eagle free of its holster, he pushed the barrel against the man's sweat-soaked forehead. "Now, you listen to me, *man.* I don't have time for games, and I will kill you without a second thought, just like I killed Spook and the Obeah man and Jacob Crisp. I need to know where the next attack is going to be, and I need to know it right now."

The Desert Eagle was a big, intimidating gun, but Bolan suspected that his words had as much of an impact as anything else. Hearing about the posse leaders being dead might have made a serious difference to this man's mind-set, because he started babbling a bit.

"I don't know, okay? We were supposed to take care of you. The big man Anders gave us lots of money to keep you out here and not by them. They have promises to keep, you know?"

"What promises?" Bolan asked.

"They promised Crisp wide-open access to Florida, didn't they? So the posse could take things in and out, and no questions asked. But that means that certain government people got to get dead and the rest need to be looking elsewhere, like Mexico. The posses love an opportunity, man."

"Where's Bailey going?'

"Where else, stupid? Florida to finish the job he started!"

"That's helpful," Bolan said. "I guess you get to live."

"Fuck you," the posse member snapped.

"But for now, you need a nap," Bolan added, lashing out with the Desert Eagle and clipping him hard enough in the temple to knock him out cold.

Local police were arriving on the scene, with their sirens and lights going full tilt. Thankful for his CIA credentials, he pulled them out as the first car arrived and held them high. He told the first officer that the men were from a Jamaican posse, and were in the United States for the sole purpose of conducting terrorist acts.

Law enforcement took both men into custody, and as soon as they'd been checked out at a hospital—assuming the badly injured man lived, since he didn't look good, Bolan noted—they'd be moved to a federal detention center until everything was settled.

By the time he'd settled the police down, Bolan knew that he'd be lucky to catch up to anyone. He eventually got into the battered car and checked his handheld computer for the new coordinates, but the GPS tracker was no longer transmitting.

He called Brognola for an update.

"What's your status, Striker?" he asked. "Do you have them or at least the precise locations of the devices?"

"No," he admitted. "I got blindsided and ended up dealing with that. The guy I locked horns with didn't know much and now the tracker has gone dead. I've got no idea where Anders and Bailey are now."

"Upload the last signal link to me and let me see if we can track it down. We can piggyback on the NSA satellite. Even if the signal is corroded, we might have a shot."

"Sounds good to me," Bolan said, sending him the information, then waiting as Brognola tried to lock down the signal.

"Hang with me, Striker..." he said. "There! The signal was traced out to Interstate 495, and somehow they managed to kill it."

"That's a big interstate, Hal," he said.

"I know, just give me a minute," Brognola said, still tapping furiously away on his computer. "Got them!" he said. "I added in the vehicle ID markers and the NSA database has them on file via traffic cams. Their last-known location was...Andrews Air Force Base."

"Then I better get a move on," Bolan said, putting the car into gear and pulling away from the wreckage of the Mustang. "I'm on my way."

The one reliable thing about traffic in the Washington, D.C., area was that it was unreliable. The gridlock that had gripped the area earlier suddenly shifted, and traffic that had been stop-and-go almost instantly became like driving in a NASCAR race. For Bolan, this meant that the drive to Andrews Air Force base only took twenty minutes, instead of an hour or more.

Andrews Air Force base was a massive compound that housed not only several air and space defense forces, but was also the home of Air Force One, the plane used by the President of the United States. Security was going to be serious, as virtually every branch of the military had facilities there. Even as he drove up, Bolan could see planes belonging to the Marines, the Navy and the Air Force. There was even insignia for the 79th Medical Wing.

As he pulled up to the security checkpoint, Bolan took his registration from the glove compartment and handed it, along with his CIA credentials, to the gate guard.

"One minute, sir," the young airman said, taking his paperwork and walking back inside the small security station.

Bolan watched as he picked up the phone. The young man

was nervous and kept looking back at him, then down at the papers clutched in his hand. Something was wrong. He'd just started to dial Brognola on his handheld computer when the car was surrounded by five gun-wielding men dressed in what could only be called Secret Service agent suits. They were practically standard issue.

"Hands where I can see them!" the closest one shouted. "Right now!"

Bolan gently put the handheld computer on his belt, then eased his hands on top of the steering wheel. An agent standing next to the car yanked open his door and grabbed him by the arm, pulling him out of the vehicle, while the others continued to keep him covered.

"Get his weapon," the man in charge said.

Bolan kept his hands up, while the man pulled out the Desert Eagle. "That's quite a cannon you're packing," he said, handing it to another man. "You always carry that much firepower?"

"Just when I'm bird hunting," Bolan said.

"Funny," the lead agent said. "Enough joking. Let's get him inside."

They began shoving him and rushing him through the security checkpoint and into the main security building with the rather innocuous label of ICC on the glass door. Made of brick, it was a relatively new facility, but Bolan knew that it was actually a large incident command center. Big enough for the daily operations required by Andrews, it could also function as a much larger ops center that could coordinate with government agencies around the globe, if a major emergency arose.

They shoved Bolan into a holding room, where the agent who'd taken his gun frisked him for additional weapons and came up empty. He retrieved Bolan's handheld computer, then put it and the Desert Eagle on the table next to the door, then stepped away far enough for the lead man to get close.

"Sit down, Agent Cooper," he said, gesturing to the table and chair in the center of the room. "I'm Agent Collins."

Agent Collins appeared to be in his late twenties, but flecks of gray were already visible along the sides of his dark hair. His eyes and body posture spoke volumes about his level of exhaustion and frustration. At the same time, there was a sense of relief to his energy. Bolan didn't have time to be detained, but knew there was nothing he could do at the moment. He'd have to play along and see what this was all about.

"Agent Collins, I'd like to know why I'm being detained," he said.

"We have credible information that you are part of a terrorist plot in the United States and that you were directly responsible for the death of Senator William Carson, his daughter Amber and several others. We have also been told that you are planning, or have planned, an assassination attempt on the President of the United States."

"That's quite a mouthful," Bolan said. "And absolutely untrue. I've been tracking those responsible for Senator Carson's death, and his daughter's, for several days now. The last lead that I have is about to slip through my fingers and you're helping him do it. You're being played by someone who knows the game very well."

"So you say," he replied. "Our sources say different."

Bolan shook his head. "Listen to me, Collins. Call Agent Mike Peterson and former Agent Robert Kowal, in Jamaica. Both of them will tell you that your information is as phony as a three-dollar bill." He took a seat in the offered chair. "I know you've got a job to do, and that any threat to the President has to be fully investigated, but the real people behind this gave me to you as a red herring."

"Why?" Collins asked. "Why you and not someone else?"

"Because I'm right on their ass," he replied, "and they're trying to buy time. There is a flight getting ready to leave

Andrews right now that is likely carrying a biological weapon that could kill thousands of people. If you want to keep me here, fine, but until this is all straightened out, you need to ground all flights going out of this base."

Agent Collins sat back and looked at Bolan in stunned amazement. "Do you honestly expect me to believe you, Agent Cooper, or whoever the hell you are?"

"What I can't figure out is why you wouldn't," he replied.

"How about the fact that in the past few days you've been everywhere the trouble has been, first in Jamaica and now in D.C. The embassy down there, along with the local police, list you as having been taken into custody, then escaping. And then you infiltrated the Pentagon!"

"I go where the leads take me," Bolan replied. "In this case, they led me to the Pentagon."

"I've run your name and credentials against the CIA active roster. Your name comes up *Agent* Cooper," Collins said, "but no case details. I think you're in up to your neck in this mess, and I think you've managed to trip up a lot of people."

"You need to trust your instincts, Collins. If you really believed all those lies, I wouldn't be in this room, talking to you, but in a deep, dark cell, somewhere," Bolan said, watching the man's reaction. When he saw that he'd struck a nerve, he continued. "I can tell that none of this feels right to you. I went into Jamaica to investigate Amber Carson's death and the bioattack that followed."

"My instincts say you're connected to this, Cooper," Collins snapped. "You're right where I'd expect to find the bad guy."

"I've got no motive," Bolan replied. "What possible reason would I have to hurt Senator Carson? I'm here in Washington chasing the bad guys, and they're right *here*. On this base. Want to detain me, that's fine. But you need to get on the phone right now and ground those planes."

"All right, then, who are we looking for?" he asked.

Bolan shook his head. "No way," he said. "Not until we're on the same team."

Shaking his head in disgust, Collins got up and left the room. Bolan sat at the table trying not to move. He knew they'd be watching him through the one-way glass, looking for any subtle clue in his body language that he was guilty. Instead of mentally counting the seconds as they ticked by, he started mentally plotting out where he thought Bailey and Anders would go once they were in Florida. There were several possibilities, since the Coast Guard patrolled the entire shoreline down there and maintained numerous bases of operation, but he was rapidly running out of options and needed to get the cavalry behind him. This was simply too big to be a one-man operation.

Collins walked back into the room. "Well, Agent Cooper, it appears that you're in luck. I just got off the phone with my watch commander and he brought me up to speed. Your story checks out."

"I thought it might," Bolan said, wondering how many strings Brognola had to pull in order to maintain his cover story.

"I've already ordered all flights grounded, but it's going to take a little time. How else can we help?"

"A short time ago, the commandant of the Coast Guard, Admiral James Bailey, and an associate, Conrad Anders, entered the base. We need to find them."

"You sure know how to aim high, Cooper," he said. He slid the Desert Eagle and the handheld computer back to Bolan. "Let's get over to the command center and see where they are."

They walked through a short, tiled hallway, then turned and passed through a security door and into a room that was filled with computer stations. One entire wall was fitted with flat-panel television screens that changed almost constantly as information was fed to them from the various people working in the room and, presumably, around the world.

Collins walked up to the law-enforcement desk and sat down at the computer station. Once he'd logged in, he punched up the flight itineraries for the base, then did a quick search by name. "Look here," he said, pointing. "Admiral Bailey's flight left five minutes ago. Anders is on a flight that's taxiing onto the tarmac right now."

"Stop that flight right now!" Bolan demanded. "I need to get out there." He spun and ran for the door as Collins shouted orders and followed behind him. They hit the main exit just as an MP driving a Jeep screeched to a stop in front of them.

Both men jumped in, and Collins barked, "Flight line, now!" The MP gunned the engine and turned on his lights and sirens. They hit the tarmac at full speed and started catching up to the plane, which had ground to a halt. As they closed the final gap, the sound of bullets ricocheting off the Jeep and the concrete forced them to skid to a stop.

All three of them hit the ground, rolling for cover at the rear of the vehicle. The jet had come to a stop, and Anders had opened the small entrance ramp and was leaning out occasionally to take shots at them with a small model assault rifle.

"I suppose you need him alive?" Collins asked, ducking as another bullet whistled overhead.

"Yes, it's the only way to stop a biological attack," he replied.

"What's your plan?"

Bolan peeked around the side of the vehicle and looked at the plane. A bullet ricocheted off the ground in front of him, kicking up chips of concrete, and he pulled his head back.

He considered the situation for a moment, then looked at Collins.

"I've got an idea," he said. "All we need is a helicopter."

The small jet was a modified Cessna Citation CJ3. Outfitted for up to six passengers, it had a range of about eighteen hundred miles, and a superb avionics system. This one sported a subdued paint job and lacked specific branch markings, but the tail number was a federal designation. Anders's plane was currently parked in the middle of the runway, surrounded by military police vehicles and enough weapons to conquer a small Central American nation. With so many terrorist threats around the world, and specifically on U.S. targets, shots fired on an Air Force base brought out the troops, literally. Armed servicemen were being staged, while hazmat and decontamination stations were being set up nearby in case the biological threat was genuine.

And Bolan needed to get to Anders before any of them. If Anders was arrested, God only knew how long it would be before he could question him.

"A helicopter?" Collins asked.

"Yes, a helicopter," he repeated. "Quickly."

"I'll play along," he said. "Come with me."

They slipped back into the crowd, and Collins gave specific orders for them to hold and not attack unless they were fired upon. Then, he climbed back into the Jeep and drove Bolan back to the command post.

It took only a few minutes to get the plan in motion and a chopper pilot brought in for a quick briefing. The pilot nodded in calm acceptance of his role in the plan, as though he did this kind of thing every day. Bolan had to admire his confidence.

Bolan and the pilot took the Jeep to a series of pads at the rear of the jet hangars, and the pilot jumped in to warm up the rescue helicopter that he'd requested. Two additional crewman jumped in the back, and one of them kicked the rescue ladder. Finding the end, Bolan placed one foot on the very last rung and wrapped his arms around another. He automatically ducked his head as the whirring blades pulsed with life, sending torrents of wind through the area.

The helicopter began to lift off the ground, pulling the slack out of the ladder. Bolan held on tight as the tension built, and finally the flexible bridge lifted him off the ground. The helicopter rising over the hangar was the signal for Collins, who'd returned to the plane, to begin shouting demands to Anders. The helicopter stayed low, using the large hangars for cover while Collins used the sirens and other vehicles to help mask the noise.

Bolan hung low on the bottom rung, using his leg much like a trapeze artist would to balance himself as they moved up and over the airplane. His original plan was to drop on top of the plane itself, but Anders chose that moment to stick his head out of the open door and peer up at the chopper.

He had to have known things were about to end badly, because he pulled his rifle from inside the plane and pointed it toward Collins and the men on the tarmac.

"No way," Bolan said. He pulled the Micro Desert Eagle from his boot, allowed himself to hang by one leg and put a round into Anders's shoulder.

The criminal stood up as he screamed and tried to lift the rifle in Bolan's direction.

Without hesitation he let go of the ladder to crash down on top of Anders. The rifle flew out of the injured man's hands as they tumbled down the steep slope of the stairs.

Despite the impact, both men hit the ground, rolled and came up ready to fight.

Bloodied, but not broken, Anders said, "Who the hell are you, really?"

"A patriot," Bolan said, closing the gap between them. Anders was too big to go high, so he went low instead, dropping at the last second to drive a booted heel into the man's knee. It made an odd popping sound as the kneecap was crushed.

Even as he started to go down, Anders swung a massive fist, connecting with Bolan's temple and coming close to knocking him out. The man hit like a mule. It took most of Bolan's will to continue the maneuver, sliding past Anders on one side, then rising to his feet behind him.

As the bigger man went down, Bolan ignored the ringing in his ears and the black flashes in his vision, and delivered a shot to the back of the traitor's neck and another to the kidney. In excruciating pain, and sucking wind, Anders went down and rolled to his back, even as Bolan pulled his Desert Eagle and aimed it directly between his eyes.

"Had enough already?" Anders gasped out. "We haven't even started yet."

Bolan fired the heavy weapon directly into the concrete next to the man's head. "We've started and stopped. You're done, Anders, and now you're going to tell me where you have devices planted in D.C."

"You think so?" Anders spit. "Why should I?"

Bolan leaned closer, shoving the barrel under his chin. "Because I won't miss next time. Talk or die, those are your choices."

"Who are you?" he asked. "If you're CIA, then I'm Papa Smurf."

"All you need to know is that I'm someone who will not hesitate to kill you, right now, in front of all these witnesses, if you don't tell me what I need to know."

Anders looked at him carefully for a long minute. "I believe you," he finally said. Then he began to outline the precise locations of where the bio bombs had been placed, including one in the Washington Monument. "That one," he said, wrapping up, "is due to go off in about an hour, in tandem with a tour of officials planning a site visit."

"All of this," Bolan said, "just to prove something that every law-enforcement agency in the world already knows? You and Bailey are crazy."

Anders shrugged. "Bailey may be. I'm in it for the money, not that it matters anymore."

"You're right about that. Where's Bailey going?"

"He's headed for the Florida Keys," he replied. "The tower will have his flight plan."

"I'm more interested in his real plan than what he filed with the tower," Bolan said. "What is it?"

"He wouldn't share it," Anders replied. "Told me he was saving the best for last."

"Fine," Bolan said. "I'm sure these other men have some questions for you. I wouldn't risk pissing them off. They might not be as understanding as I am."

Bolan backed off Anders as the cavalry started moving in on them. Holstering his weapon, he turned and stepped forward to meet Collins. He heard the sound of a weapon cocking, and the sixth sense that had developed after years of being in deadly situations warned him to hit the dirt.

He did, executing a spinning roll to his left, and brought around the Desert Eagle in the same motion. His first shot was only a half second behind those of Collins and several MPs, who had seen Anders get to his feet and draw the weapon from behind his back. The blast from the bullets lifted Anders into the air and back onto the ramp to the plane, bleeding in several places. He twitched once or twice, then died.

Collins ran forward to help Bolan as he levered himself off the ground.

"You all right?" he asked. "That was one hell of a stunt you pulled."

"I'll feel it all later, I'm certain," Bolan said tersely, aware of how close to death he'd just come. "Right now I need a fast flight to Florida."

"Well," Collins said, "you're on an Air Force base, so I think we can help."

"Good," Bolan said. "While you arrange that, I've got a call to make to ensure that those weapons are contained."

"Mind if I ask one question?" he said.

"Shoot," he replied.

"I heard him—Anders—ask who you really are. It's sort of on my mind, too."

"Like I told him," Bolan said, "I'm a patriot." He turned away then, pulling his handheld computer from his belt to call Brognola and stop the threat to the city of D.C. from the weapons planted by Anders. By the time he was done, Collins had his flight arranged.

It was time to stop the mastermind behind this mess once and for all.

RATHER THAN TRY to find a new plane, Collins had the clever idea of simply using the same Cessna Citation that Anders was going to use. After a quick search turned up a briefcase and a laptop belonging to the man, a new crew was assigned, and Bolan and Collins both were quickly on board and in flight. According to the logs, Anders had landed in Key West little more than an hour and a half behind Bailey's own flight.

En route, they had tried to reach the Coast Guard Command Center, but it seemed they were conducting some sort of coastal emergency drill, which caused information to be bogged down and no real messages were getting through. Despite the fact that Bailey was clearly misguided and willing to break the law, Bolan had to give the man kudos for thinking fast on his feet. So far, he hadn't missed too many tricks, and he'd been a step or more ahead the entire time. Bolan was determined to put an end to that situation immediately.

Collins had arranged for an MP to meet them at the airstrip, and the drive over to the Coast Guard base took only a few minutes. They arrived at the main gate to discover that the base was in complete lockdown mode. It wasn't a particularly large facility, comprised of maybe a dozen different ships, along with hangars for sea and rescue aircraft. The compound itself was surrounded by fence on the landward side, and the piers would be heavily guarded.

"This guy is an expert at roadblocks," Collins said.

"He's thought it through pretty carefully," Bolan agreed. "Let's see about getting in there."

They approached the young ensign standing guard, who came to attention and said, "Halt!" in his most authoritative voice. He looked to be about a week out of officer school, with a fringe of blond hair and blue eyes that were serious, but lacked any experience.

If the young man's voice hadn't cracked on a higher register, Bolan might have even taken him seriously. "At ease," he said. He showed the young man his CIA credentials. "I'm Agent Cooper, this is Special Agent Collins from the Secret Service. We need to get onto the base."

"I'm sorry, sir," the ensign said. "We're on lockdown for a drill. I can't let anyone onto the grounds until that's over and Captain Cline gives the all clear."

"Then let us speak to Captain Cline," Collins said.

"I'm sorry, sir," he said. "The captain is participating in the drill and not available. It should all be over in a half hour or so, if you'd like to wait."

"We're running out of time here," Bolan growled. "Who ordered this drill?"

"Sir?"

"*Who* ordered the drill?" he repeated.

"The drill was ordered by Coast Guard Commandant James Bailey," he said. "It was a surprise to us, but readiness inspections aren't all that uncommon."

"When?" Collins asked.

"This morning, sir," the ensign said. "About 0930."

"Listen," Bolan said. "In about half an hour, this base is going to be crawling with Secret Service agents, the CDC, the FBI and, for all I know, the FDA. Admiral Bailey is a traitor, and he's using this base and the Coast Guard to cover up his illegal activities. We aren't going to let him get away with it, and if you make us stand out here waiting for this so-called drill to be over, he will."

"Sir?" the ensign said, visibly shaken.

"And," he added, "I will personally see to it that you get the blame."

"So this isn't part of the drill, sir?"

"No, the drill is just a cover that Bailey is using. There is no drill. This is all real life, and if I don't get some help it's going to turn into a real-life disaster."

The young ensign thought it over, then nodded.

"Now," Bolan said, "I'm going to need your help."

After opening the pedestrian gate, Bolan and Collins followed the young ensign inside, and he led them across a parking area to a small security building. He went in to ring the captain.

"I think it's going to take both of us to convince Captain Cline that we're not crazy," Collins whispered to Bolan.

"It's hard to believe that a superior officer is a traitor," he replied. "A tough pill to swallow, especially if it's the man at the very top of the food chain."

They didn't have to wait long to get a response, nor did they have to go and find Captain Cline. He was storming his way toward them. At six four, he towered over most of the crew and didn't look as if he was in the mood to hear wild stories. In fact, he didn't really look as if he was *ever* in the mood to hear stories.

"Here we go," Collins muttered.

"What in the hell is going on here?" he yelled as he reached them. "This is my goddamn base, and if we want to run a drill, or lock the base down or ride ATVs on the piers, then by God, we'll do it."

Bolan took a deep breath, preparing to do verbal battle,

but Collins beat him to it. "Would you feel that way, Captain, if we were acting on direct orders from the President of the United States?"

After a long moment of staring hard at the two men, he nodded. "Ensign, return to your post. We're still on lockdown until I say different."

He turned to Bolan and Collins. "You two, come with me."

They followed him across the parking lot and into the building where his office was located. He opened the door and pointed to two chairs on the other side of his desk, then sat down in his own. Bolan scanned the sparsely furnished office quickly, noting the family pictures that depicted a rather large clan of children, all of them holding various kinds of guns and looking as if they were getting ready to go on a hunting trip.

"Now, gentlemen, tell me what's going on," Cline said. "And it better be good."

Collins nodded at Bolan to give the explanation. "The short version, Captain, is that Admiral Bailey is directly responsible for the deaths of Senator William Carson and his daughter, and a number of other people down in Jamaica."

"The commandant of the Coast Guard—*my* Coast Guard—is a killer?" Cline said, his voice rising in disbelief. "That's some story."

"He's in possession of a rather unique form of weaponized Anthrax, Captain," Collins said. "He's used it in several attacks and is planning for more. All to prove a point about our border security."

"He's got a point about our border security," Captain Cline said. "I've heard him speak on it, but if what you're saying is true, that's no way to prove it."

"It's true," Collins said. "What's more, he's no longer the commandant. The President is taking care of that right now."

"And we need to take care of him," Bolan added. "Before anyone else gets hurt."

Captain Cline sat back and looked at the two men in front of him. "And you two are 150 percent certain this is for real?"

"It's deadly real," Bolan said. "Now where is he?"

"As of ten minutes or so ago, he was in the helo hangar. After he ordered the drill, he informed me that he was going to come down and participate himself. A little unusual, but something he's been known to do from time to time."

Bolan leaned forward intently. "In what capacity was he going to participate?"

"We've been running some joint maneuvers with the British navy," he said. "Admiral Bailey was going to play the role of an aggressive helicopter trying to land on the base."

"That explains the Super Lynx," Bolan said.

"Sure, we've got them here as part of the exercises. Why?"

"I saw one in Jamaica," he replied. "Is Bailey familiar with them?"

"He set up the joint exercise," Cline admitted. He picked up the phone on his desk. "I'll send a security team to the hangar now and have him detained."

"No, don't," Bolan said.

"Why the hell not?" the captain responded.

"Because we don't want to take the chance of him dispersing the anthrax and having even more victims," Collins said. "Who knows what kind of device he's got with him?"

"So what do you want me to do?" Cline asked. "Wait and hope?"

Bolan shook his head. "No, I want you to set up a perimeter. Agent Collins and I will go in and take him down."

"We will?" Collins asked, looking a bit pale. "I thought you..."

"You wanted to come along," Bolan reminded him. "That means you get the whole ride—unless you want out."

"No," Collins said, then turned back to the captain. "Let's get this party started. We don't want to keep the admiral waiting."

Captain Cline picked up his desk phone and began barking orders.

DESPITE HIS RATHER large stature and loud voice, Captain Cline proved to be a man of subtlety. He got the perimeter of the helicopter hangar completely surrounded in almost total silence.

"How many men are inside the hangar?" Bolan asked.

"We passed the word quietly," Cline replied. "I think we've got about a half dozen inside still. The rest left using different excuses."

"Bailey has got to be suspicious by now," Collins said. "He has to know that we took down Anders."

Bolan considered it, then nodded. "It's likely," he admitted. "We've still got to go in and get him."

Before either of them could form an attack plan, however, the main hangar doors exploded in a massive ball of fire. Men yelled and hit the deck, seeking cover wherever it was available.

"What the hell was that?" Collins shouted over the noise, as they ducked behind a Jeep.

"Rocket," Bolan said. "He knows we're here."

Inside the hangar, the sound of a helicopter's rotors turning could be heard. "And he's making a run for it," Collins said. "Damn."

"Captain, tell your men to fall back," Bolan said. "No point in giving him targets. He wants out of the hangar, so let him out."

"And then what?" Collins asked. "He'll take off."

"He'll head out to sea," Bolan corrected, "and away from all these people. I'll take him there."

Nearby, Captain Cline used a bullhorn and ordered his men to retreat. From inside the hangar, Bolan could tell that the chopper was ready to leave and sure enough, a moment later, the glass-covered cockpit of a UK Naval Super Lynx cleared the doors. It took Bailey another minute to be completely out and rising slowly into the sky.

Bolan jumped to his feet and ran for the hangar. Collins was right on his heels. "Where are you going?" Cline called.

"Just going to borrow a chopper, Captain," Bolan yelled. "I'll bring it back."

"The hell you are!" he roared.

At that moment, the perimeter alarms for the base began to wail. Bolan and Collins got into the hangar and skidded to a stop. Two more of the same helicopter model were inside. "Okay," Bolan said, "I'm going after Bailey, and you're going to stay here and do damage control."

"Why?" Collins asked. "I can help."

"You know how to fly a combat chopper?" Bolan asked.

"No."

"Right, but I do. And besides, Captain Cline is going into cardiac arrest right now. I'm guessing those perimeter alarms are the cavalry. You're going to have to deal with them, get me clear skies and be ready to come to my rescue if it all goes to hell."

Collins nodded. "I'll handle it," he said. "Just go get the son of a bitch."

"Count on it," Bolan said, then he turned and climbed into one of the choppers. The Super Lynx was a multipurpose helicopter. It could be used for antisurface warfare, antisubmarine operations, and even search and rescue. These particular aircraft appeared to be the Super Lynx 300 model, which Bolan had seen used to great effect in hot zones in the Middle East as well as parts of Indonesia.

Armed with 12.7-mm door-mounted heavy machine guns, guided rockets, 20-mm cannon pods, as well as air-to-surface missiles and depth charges, it was a flying machine of death and destruction. Bolan imagined that the Coast Guard might find it useful when dealing with the increasingly violent drug smugglers working off the southern tip of the United States.

He fired up the rotors and quickly got under way, bringing the sensor suite online. It was a full-array sensor, called a Seaspray 7000, which offered 360-degree coverage. Bolan was able to spot Bailey's chopper almost immediately, and he poured on the speed to close the distance.

Over his headset, he heard Collins's voice come on. "Cooper, do you copy?"

"I copy," he replied. "Go ahead."

"You need to watch your ass out there," he said. "Bailey is still a certified combat pilot for helos, and according to his file, he has been running training missions regularly for the past few years. He knows what he's doing."

"Thanks for the heads-up," Bolan said. "I've got him on radar now and—"

His eyes narrowed as he heard the sound of machine guns opening up. Without thinking, he pulled hard on the stick, pushing left and climbing.

"Cooper? Cooper?"

"Not now," he said, going into combat mode. How Bailey had managed to sneak up on him he'd never know. He leveled out and spun the chopper in a tight circle, but didn't catch sight of Bailey.

Bolan turned back to the radar display. "What the hell?" he said to himself. Bailey's helicopter was gone. "That's impossible."

When he'd been playing catch-up, they'd been heading south by southwest, so Bolan moved out in that direction, hoping that maybe something was wrong with the sensor array. He'd no sooner gotten moving forward again than the sounds of the heavy machine guns ratcheted through the air once again.

"How's he doing that?" Bolan yelled, pushing the stick hard forward, and sending the chopper into a dive.

"Agent Cooper?" a voice came over his headset.

"This is Cooper," he said, reaching the deck about fifteen feet above the water and leveling out.

"We're tracking from shore, sir. He's using your own sensor array to hide. The signals are on the same wave frequency—bouncing off each other basically—and he's getting close enough that you can't see him."

"How do I fix that?" he asked, banking left and listening for the sound of the guns.

"You need to switch over to heads-up, sir, and turn off the sensor suite," came the reply.

"I'll give it a try," Bolan said. He flicked the switches toggling off the sensor suite, then turned on the heads-up display. It used a different set of radar systems to project data directly onto the glass canopy of the chopper.

Almost immediately, he could see Bailey's helicopter again. The Super Lynx 300 was closing in from behind and above him. Bolan began to slowly drop speed, easing back a little bit at a time. What he was doing was risky, but it didn't seem as if he had any choice. The man knew a lot more tricks about air combat than he did.

He watched Bailey's chopper closing the distance. The heads-up display noted that he was also speeding up on his approach. Bolan waited, gritting his teeth and hoping that he'd get the timing right.

He eased back a little more on the throttle. Bailey came closer, and the heads-up display started to go wild. MISSILE LOCK! MISSILE LOCK! showed red on the screen. Bolan counted silently to five, then yanked hard on the stick, lifting almost straight up in the air. He gave it all the chopper had to build speed.

Beneath him, a missile splashed into the water and exploded just beneath the surface. Directly behind it, Bailey flew through the spray, firing his machine guns.

Bolan dropped back down behind him and went weapons-hot. He got a weapons lock almost immediately, and Bailey knew it. He began flying erratically, trying to get clear. But there was no way Bolan was going to lose him this time.

He flicked on an open communications channel. "Admiral Bailey, this is Agent Matt Cooper. You are ordered to stand down and return to base."

"I can't do that, Agent Cooper," he replied. "My mission isn't over."

"It is over, Admiral," he said. "Turn off your weapons systems and return to base immediately, or you will force me to fire."

Bailey banked the chopper back toward land. "You won't shoot me down," he said. "I'm the commandant of the United States Coast Guard!"

"Admiral, this is your last warning," Bolan said. "Turn off your weapon systems immediately."

The only reply was mad laughter, and Bolan knew he had little choice. If Bailey had somehow put the anthrax into one of the missiles, or even just crashed into the base itself, a lot of people could and probably would die. "Ten seconds, Admiral," he said.

"You won't do it! They'll eat you alive in D.C. for killing me!"

Bolan thought they might…if they could find him, which didn't seem all that likely. In the distance, he could see the coastline and the faint outlines of the buildings on the Coast Guard base. It was enough. He made his decision.

"Goodbye, Admiral Bailey," he said. Then he fired two missiles. With a hard lock, it would have been almost impossible to miss, but he nearly did. Bailey tried to cut hard right and the first missile only tagged the landing gear, but the impact was enough to turn the chopper in midair.

Bolan got a split-second look at the man's face as the second missile slammed into the side of his chopper. A macabre grin of horror lit his eyes, then nothing as the helicopter exploded in the air.

Bolan climbed slightly and watched as the pieces fell into the ocean. Whatever anthrax was aboard would be lost in the ocean or in the explosion forever.

"Cooper?" Collins called over the radio. "What's your status?"

"Send out a recovery boat," he said, "to pick up the pieces and find Admiral Bailey's body."

There was a long moment of silence, then Collins said, "They're on their way. Good work."

Bolan shook his head. There was nothing good about killing a man like Bailey except to protect the lives of others. The admiral had given his entire life to his country and when it finally drove him mad, he tried to protect it the only way he thought he could. In the depths of his madness, he'd lost his way.

It wasn't all that difficult to understand really. Not for a man like Bolan, and not for a man who had killed for his country so many times he'd lost count. And for a man called the Executioner, justice like this was sometimes necessary, but it would never be anything more than icy-cold comfort.

Bolan banked the helicopter back toward the coastline. He'd leave it somewhere they could find it, but before they did, he would disappear once more. He knew it wouldn't be long until his country needed him again, but for the time being, the shores were safe.

* * * * *

Don Pendleton

TERMINAL GUIDANCE

A fresh wave of terror is unleashed across the Middle East...

U.S. intelligence agencies are picking up chatter about something big coming their way. When a series of calculated executions of undercover intelligence personnel occur in key cities, the Oval Office is convinced this is the attack the world has feared. The Stony Man teams deploy to the hot spots, seeking to smash a deadly alliance of terror....

STONY MAN®

Available December wherever books are sold.

Or order your copy now by sending your name, address, zip or postal code, along with a check or money order (please do not send cash) for $6.99 for each book ordered ($7.99 in Canada), plus 75¢ postage and handling ($1.00 in Canada), payable to Gold Eagle Books, to:

In the U.S.
Gold Eagle Books
3010 Walden Avenue
P.O. Box 9077
Buffalo, NY 14269-9077

In Canada
Gold Eagle Books
P.O. Box 636
Fort Erie, Ontario
L2A 5X3

Please specify book title with your order.
Canadian residents add applicable federal and provincial taxes.

www.readgoldeagle.blogspot.com

GSM116

Assassin's Code

The Big Easy becomes a playground of destruction...

There's a brutal new player in the Middle East—a mysterious group of radicalized assassins has unleashed havoc. When a U.S. envoy is slaughtered, Mack Bolan picks up the hunt in the Afghan mountains, the first leg of a mission to stem the flow of spilled blood across a shattered region...and the world.

Available December wherever books are sold.

Or order your copy now by sending your name, address, zip or postal code, along with a check or money order (please do not send cash) for $6.99 for each book ordered ($7.99 in Canada), plus 75¢ postage and handling ($1.00 in Canada), payable to Gold Eagle Books, to:

In the U.S.
Gold Eagle Books
3010 Walden Avenue
P.O. Box 9077
Buffalo, NY 14269-9077

In Canada
Gold Eagle Books
P.O. Box 636
Fort Erie, Ontario
L2A 5X3

Please specify book title with your order.
Canadian residents add applicable federal and provincial taxes.

www.readgoldeagle.blogspot.com

GSB146

TAKE 'EM FREE

2 action-packed novels plus a mystery bonus

NO RISK

NO OBLIGATION TO BUY

SPECIAL LIMITED-TIME OFFER

Mail to: The Reader Service

IN U.S.A.: P.O. Box 1867, Buffalo, NY 14240-1867
IN CANADA: P.O. Box 609, Fort Erie, Ontario L2A 5X3

YEAH! Rush me 2 FREE Gold Eagle® novels and my FREE mystery bonus (bonus is worth about $5). If I don't cancel, I will receive 6 hot-off-the-press novels every other month. Bill me at the low price of just $31.94 for each shipment.* That's a savings of at least 24% off the combined cover prices and there is NO extra charge for shipping and handling! There is no minimum number of books I must buy. I can always cancel at any time simply by returning a shipment at your cost or by returning any shipping statement marked "cancel." Even if I never buy another book, the 2 free books and mystery bonus are mine to keep forever.

166/366 ADN FEJF

Name (PLEASE PRINT)

Address Apt. #

City State/Prov. Zip/Postal Code

Signature (if under 18, parent or guardian must sign)

Not valid to current subscribers of Gold Eagle books.
Want to try two free books from another series?
Call 1-800-873-8635 or visit www.ReaderService.com.

* Terms and prices subject to change without notice. Prices do not include applicable taxes. Sales tax applicable in N.Y. Canadian residents will be charged applicable taxes. Offer not valid in Quebec. This offer is limited to one order per household. All orders subject to credit approval. Credit or debit balances in a customer's account(s) may be offset by any other outstanding balance owed by or to the customer. Please allow 4 to 6 weeks for delivery. Offer available while quantities last.

Your Privacy—The Reader Service is committed to protecting your privacy. Our Privacy Policy is available online at www.ReaderService.com or upon request from the Reader Service.

We make a portion of our mailing list available to reputable third parties that offer products we believe may interest you. If you prefer that we not exchange your name with third parties, or if you wish to clarify or modify your communication preferences, please visit us at www.ReaderService.com/consumerschoice or write to us at Reader Service Preference Service, P.O. Box 9062, Buffalo, NY 14269. Include your complete name and address.

GE11B

JAMES AXLER
DEATH LANDS®
Lost Gates

A deadly cult goes on a killing spree in Detroit...

Baron Crabbe is dangerously high on legends of the Trader and rumors of a secret cache. His ace in the hole is Ryan Cawdor and his band—his prisoners. Ryan knows the truth, and it won't help Crabbe, but the only option is to play along with the crazed baron's scheme. Staying alive is all about buying time—waiting for their one chance to chill their captors.

Available November 2011 wherever books are sold.

Or order your copy now by sending your name, address, zip or postal code, along with a check or money order (please do not send cash) for $6.99 for each book ordered ($7.99 in Canada), plus 75¢ postage and handling ($1.00 in Canada), payable to Gold Eagle Books, to:

In the U.S.
Gold Eagle Books
3010 Walden Avenue
P.O. Box 9077
Buffalo, NY 14269-9077

In Canada
Gold Eagle Books
P.O. Box 636
Fort Erie, Ontario
L2A 5X3

Please specify book title with your order.
Canadian residents add applicable federal and provincial taxes.

www.readgoldeagle.blogspot.com

GDL101

2442

James Axler
Outlanders®

INFESTATION CUBED

Earth's saviors are on the run as more nightmares descend upon Earth...

Ullikummis, the would-be cruel master of Earth, has captured Brigid Baptiste, luring Kane and Grant on a dangerous pursuit. All while pan-terrestrial scientists conduct a horrifying experiment in parasitic mind control. But true evil has yet to reveal itself, as the alliance scrambles to regroup—before humankind loses its last and only hope.

Available November wherever books are sold.

Or order your copy now by sending your name, address, zip or postal code, along with a check or money order (please do not send cash) for $6.99 for each book ordered ($7.99 in Canada), plus 75¢ postage and handling ($1.00 in Canada), payable to Gold Eagle Books, to:

In the U.S.
Gold Eagle Books
3010 Walden Avenue
P.O. Box 9077
Buffalo, NY 14269-9077

In Canada
Gold Eagle Books
P.O. Box 636
Fort Erie, Ontario
L2A 5X3

GOLD EAGLE®

Please specify book title with your order.
Canadian residents add applicable federal and provincial taxes.

www.readgoldeagle.blogspot.com

GOUT59